The Diary

David Dodd

North
Country
Press

ISBN 978-1-943424-26-9

Library of Congress Control Number: 2017913777

Cover photo by Lisa L. Jackson

The Diary

September 7, 1961, was a very, very important day in my life. That was two days ago and the world, as I know it, will be changed forever because of the mistake I made on that day. Just why I'm writing this down today I truly do not know. I guess it's my way of trying to explain what happened from my point of view. I realize that by documenting this activity that I surely am putting myself at grave risk.

I can't stop thinking about my family and how they'll deal with this whole mess. My seven-year-old sister will not believe what I did. My twenty-two-year-old brother, now working and out on his own, will hate what I've done and I'm sure be ashamed of me. The deepest cut of all though will be when my mom finds out. She has raised us kids on her own since Dad died four years ago in a winter car accident. Mid-coast Maine roads at times are very treacherous and Dad found that out, the hard way. It will break Mom's heart if she ever finds out. To tell the truth I have even strongly considered suicide during the last couple of days. I couldn't do that! The family has had a tough enough history as is and I should not make it even worse by taking the easy way out by ending my life.

I did go out for a short time this afternoon and went to the soda shop downtown to see if anyone had gotten wind of my felony yet. The shop is the best place in town to get all of the local gossip and news. One of my best friends, Steve Morrissey, was there sitting at the soda fountain and he was telling everyone about a strange occurrence that had happened several nights ago. Apparently, Steve had been tenting as he often did in the summer months and this time he had pitched his tent in the woods down behind our high school. Steve's tent was a couple hundred feet into the woods where nobody could see or bother him. It had gotten to be about 9:00 p.m. and he had just finished a snack and was climbing into his sleeping bag when he heard a loud noise crashing through the trees behind him. It sounded like someone had thrown something into the woods. He immediately jumped out of his sleeping bag and quickly ran out to the field that lay directly behind our high school. He said that he spotted someone running at quite a distance on the other side of the field. Steve said that for a moment he thought about following the person to see who he or she was, but decided not to as the individual disappeared behind the junior high school that sits directly beside our high school. Steve told me that he was going to be busy the following day as he was testing to see if he could become a law enforcement officer but if I wanted to join him the next day we could go down behind the school to see if we could locate what the crashing had been behind him that night. I have decided to go to school and carry on my life as normally as I can, for a while anyway, and I told Steve I'd meet him at 3:00 p.m. two days hence and we could scout out the high school woods area.

9/11/61

Rain, rain, rain and fog today, but that did not prevent the search. I met Steve as planned behind the school and he began, intently, to search for what had been apparently thrown into the woods behind his camping spot. I followed close behind him with great interest. He felt we'd have to search at least an acre of land unless we got lucky and spotted our prize early. The dense trees and bushes along with the soggy underpinning of the woods floor made our efforts more difficult. It took almost an hour but Steve finally found what he was searching for. In the crotch of a medium-sized hardwood tree he spotted a small burlap bag. Steve thought this must be what had been thrown that night and he stated he was glad no one had found it prior to us. He shinned up the tree and grabbed the sack, then, off-balanced, dropped to the ground. The sack was tied at the top and was heavier than it had appeared up in the tree. I will always remember the look on Steve's face when a long-barreled Smith and Wesson 22 caliber pistol fell out of the bag in front of him. He was incredulous that someone had thrown such a fine pistol away. But, Steve is very savvy and as we walked out of the woods he stated that this weapon just might have been involved in a crime. He told me that he would take the pistol home and we could later decide what should be done with it. I got home just before supper and my mom gave me a hug and asked how my day had been.

9/13/61

Today started out to be a truly boring day. I did go to school, but I can only remember one thing that happened. I met a very nice girl that had just transferred to our school from the Portland area. She never told me her name, but I will make a point to see her again I'm sure. After school I walked home and arrived here at about 3:15 p.m. Man was I surprised when I opened the front door and stepped inside! My mom, my brother and my sister were standing right in front of me and they were singing happy birthday. I had totally forgotten that indeed, yes, this is my birthday! They hugged and kissed me and we all had a piece of cake as well as ice cream to top it off. I realized that Mom could not afford to buy me the 22 caliber Mossberg rifle that she gave me, but it is my first gun and there was just no way that I couldn't accept her gift. My brother had asked to leave his job early so he could be there and little sis was by my side for the whole evening. As I turn out my bedroom light tonight I realize that the way my family treated me today has strengthened my resolve to not admit to doing what I did. I just do not have the heart to hurt my family, especially my mom and little sis. I'll have to bear the burden of my deed, at least for now. I'm sixteen years old now. I hope that I'll be able to overcome the funk that I've been in. I hope that I'll be able to survive.

9/14/61

Today the news that hit the airwaves was perhaps the biggest news ever released since the Civil War, at least for our little town. Rance Edwards' body had been found up at his hunting camp which is located up in the mountains which run adjacent to our village. He had been shot and was dead. The reports indicated that at press time it had not been determined if the death was a suicide or a murder. This might not have been quite as important news had Rance not been one of the key people, not only in our town, but also was key in our county and state as well. He was owner and CEO of the only mill in town and he had 400 or more employees working for him. That made him important and made him the employer with the most employees in the county. My mother is one of those employees. To the public he seemed to be a personable and hard-working individual. He was still young, being only 42 years old, and was contemplating running for political office in the future. Rance seemed to be a very nice young man, but to those who really knew him he was a tyrant. There was talk over the years by several female employees, that he ended up firing, that he had made unwanted advances towards them. This had never been proven and no legal actions had been taken and no reports had ever been released in the press concerning those allegations. The only way I knew about this is that I had heard a couple of my high school classmates joking about it in the men's room one day at school. I didn't know whether to believe it or not at the time. Rance's body was taken from the camp and sent over to our state capital, Augusta, to have an autopsy done on it. It was reported that it might take several weeks before it could be determined what had actually occurred. Rance had apparently been on vacation and nobody had noticed his absence.

9/15/61

Steve Morrissey called me this evening and told me that because of Rance's recent demise he had decided to take the pistol that we had found to the sheriff's department post haste. He also related to me that he had been hired, on a temporary basis to start with, by the sheriff's department as a deputy. I'm very proud of Steve for this accomplishment and I'm sure he will reach full-time status with them in short order. He told me that a weapon had been found on the floor of Rance's camp near the dead body, but to be safe he had delivered the pistol, still enclosed in the burlap sack, to the sheriff today. He felt that the activities of the weapon thrower had been rather unusual that evening and he related the strange occurrence to the sheriff and his head deputy. They both found it to be very strange as well and said that they would be checking into it as soon as possible. Steve said he would start his new job next week as one of the deputies was about to retire. At only nineteen years of age Steve is one of the youngest employees ever hired by the sheriff's dept. Usually a new employee is hired to work the switchboard, but Steve's high school record was at a high level and he has never had any trouble with the law so he really was quite an easy hire by the dept. I have not been sleeping well since I made my mistake. I also have cried several times after going to bed and turning the lights out recently. My little sister came into my bedroom to kiss me goodnight and she saw tears in my eyes. I kissed her and sent her back to her room and told her everything was alright. I do not like to lie to anyone and dislike it even more lying to my little sister who is the light of my life......

9/19/61

Nothing of note has happened over the past few days, at least not in our little town. On the wider front, I saw Nikita Khrushchev's face today on the cover of *Time* magazine. The image reeked of hate. I didn't bother to read the article about him. Oh, I did go to the movie a couple of nights ago with a classmate and he and I watched *West Side Story* which had just been released. We both enjoyed it very much although there was much hate to be seen in it. The final scene of the movie is very powerful. Although one of the lead characters, Tony, had been gunned down and was dead I noticed that the two rival gangs joined as one, at the show's finale, and lifted Tony's body and carried it away as the movie ended. There is great, great music in this film! I feel that when the two gangs put aside their differences and out of respect joined to help move Tony's body that hopefully this will be an important sign for the whole world to see. Yes, no matter how much past negativity is between factions, we can come together and maybe learn to coexist in peace and harmony.

9/24/61

Today we had an assembly in the gymnasium at school and some of the town's firefighters gave a presentation to show us what we should and shouldn't do in case we had a fire there at school or in our homes. All of the students were seated on the bleachers and I was sitting next to my friend, Jack Perry. Out of the corner of my eye I happened to get a glimpse of the new girl in town. She was sitting down below where Jack and I were seated. She looked very nice and, actually, she always does. After the presentation was over Jack and I followed her and her friends back up the hallways to our classroom area. I had told Jack that I thought that this girl is really cute and he agreed. What happened next I will never forget. As she turned to her left to go into her next class she glanced behind her and immediately focused on my eyes. Wow!! Then, while going through the door she smiled at me. I think that I smiled back at her and probably said "Hi" or something stupid like that, but I really can't remember if I did or not. I know now even more than I knew before that I will have to approach her soon and hopefully get to know her. When I got home my sister was playing in her room and my mom had supper cooking. Her eyes were red and it looked like she had been crying. I asked her what the problem was and she told me that she was upset that Rance had died. She told me that she really didn't like the man, but he had been her employer for many years so it was natural for her to feel this way. She said that she hoped it would be released by the law enforcement soon just how he had died. I turned the burners down on the stove as the food was starting to cook onto the pans.

9/27/61

Today the sheriff made an abbreviated statement to the press outside of the sheriff's office. He stated that the autopsy that had been done on Rance's body had revealed that the death was now being considered a homicide. Several of the reporters tried to ask Sheriff Dolloff questions, but Dolloff would not release any further information and he quickly returned to his department. His announcement, though brief, was reported on our local tv stations and that is where I saw it this evening. I made sure that little sis, Terri, was upstairs and would not hear the gory news. After a few minutes I came downstairs and saw that Mom had been crying again. She felt that Rance being murdered was even worse than if he had committed suicide. She was really shook up. Later we went off to bed, but I don't think she will get much rest tonight.

10/1/61

I happened to run into Steve at the soda shop today. I ordered my usual, vanilla cola, and sat down at a table with him. He told me things were going well at his new job and that the sheriff was keeping him very busy. I told him that I have an eye on the new girl that just moved to our town. He stated that he knew her as she lives on the same street that he does. He told me that I should go for it and introduce myself to her. He agreed with me that she was very attractive. I told him that I'd try to get my courage up. He told me that he had an idea how I could meet her. Steve told me that this Saturday night there was going to be an end of summer dance at the local dance hall and if I would come he'd be glad to introduce me to her. He said that he had met her and that she was a very nice young lady. I told him that I'd be very nervous in meeting her, but that I'd be there. He also stated that he wanted very much for Rance's killer to be caught and brought to justice. He said that the whole department was doing everything possible to make sure that the crime did not go unsolved. I told Steve that I'd meet him at the dance at about 7:00 p.m. He told me that the girl's name is Sally Slater.

10/6/61

Well I did show up for the dance tonight which was really strange because (1) I don't know how to dance and (2) I was really nervous about meeting Sally. I walked into the dance hall and a country and western band was entertaining. Later I was glad that it had been a C&W band playing tonight as, to me, rock bands seem harder to dance to. I scanned the hall with my eyes and did not see Steve yet. I did see Sally over on the far side of the hall and she was talking with a few of her female friends. I waited at the entrance and in a few minutes Steve showed up. He seemed in high spirits and asked me if I wanted him to introduce Sally to me. I did not want to appear to be afraid so I agreed that there was no time like the present. We walked across the dance floor and Steve tapped Sally on her back and stated he had someone that he'd like to introduce to her. He made the introduction and, although I tried to look as confident as possible, I truly was a nervous wreck inside. Unbelievably we hit it off right from the start. I suggested that we go over to the snack tables and have a soda. She walked with me and I bought a drink for each of us and we stood for a while watching the dancers and listening to the band. Sally seemed to somehow sense that I was not a dancer and she asked if I wanted her to show me how to dance. Still putting on a brave front I nodded yes and she took me by the hand and lead me onto the floor to down near where the band was playing. Luckily the first song we tried to dance to was a slow waltz and the lights were very low so I hope that it covered up my inadequacy. To save me I can't remember what the first song we danced to was. All I do remember is that the whole evening was wonderful! She seems to like me and to say that I feel the same towards her would be an understatement. She did dance with a few other fellows tonight, but we spent the majority of the evening together and we danced the final dance of the night with each other. I offered to walk her home and she said okay, but that she'd have to call her parents to let them know that they didn't have to come to pick her up. She made her call and we said goodnight to our friends and I walked her home which is only a few blocks from the dance hall. As I left her at her doorway she told me that she had a wonderful time and hoped to see me more often in the future. She smiled at me and I did not try to get a goodnight kiss. I felt that it was too early to try to do that and I hope that she felt the same. After she had gone inside I ran down her driveway and all the way to my house. My mom and sister were already asleep and at 11:30 p.m. I jumped into my bed and thought to myself that this was certainly one of the happiest days of my life.

10/7/61

I saw Sally a couple of times today in the school hallway between classes. We did not get a chance to speak, but she did look really nice. I waved at her both times that I saw her and she waved back and smiled from ear to ear. I have an idea that her family has a little more money than mine does as she always is dressed in really nice stylish clothing. I think that I'll call her on the phone some evening real soon as I want to get to know her better. I believe that someone told me that her dad is in the real estate business. I saw him and Sally's mom just briefly as I dropped her off at her house after the dance. I did not get a chance to talk to them however. I hope that I'll get to meet them soon.

10/12/61

Not much of note happened today. I sometimes feel that life is passing me by so, so swiftly. I'm trying to enjoy it as much as possible, but I realize that these good days will pass into history, and later on in life I'm almost sure that my time will drag slowly and be filled with monotony. The most memorable thing that happened to me was the hug Mom gave me when I got home.

10/13/61

Coach Reeves asked me to come see him after school today in the gym. I had no idea what he wanted to talk to me about and I worried about it for most of the day. I met him there at about 3:00 p.m. and we were alone and conversed on the gym floor. He told me that the varsity basketball team had fallen onto tough times and they could really use my help if I wanted to join the team. He has been the varsity coach for many years and is highly respected by his peers as his teams have always been great and they have won many district titles and a few state titles as well. I thought for a minute and then asked him how soon he needed my decision. He told me that yesterday would do and we both laughed and I told him I'd think it over tonight and I'd give him my answer tomorrow. I thanked him very much for thinking that highly of me. I have never played in any organized sports league and if I do join the team it will be a first for me. As I walked home tonight I had a pretty good idea what my decision would be, but I'll think it over in bed tonight and tell Coach what I decide to do tomorrow.

10/14/61

As I walked to school today I pretty much knew what I'd give Coach as my answer, but I was still thinking it over. He had, in asking me, given me a big compliment and I really wanted to help the team out if I could. Also, Sally Slater was a member of the cheering squad and I realized that if I joined the team I would be able to see her more. I thought and thought all day in my classes and really couldn't concentrate on much else. I went back and forth as to what my final decision would be. There were many pros to deciding to join the team and not really as many cons. Finally, during my last period class I made my decision. After going to my home room to pick up my books I trundled down the long hallway to the gymnasium and Coach was there cleaning the gym floor. I told him that I was very sorry, but for personal reasons I would not be able to take him up on his offer. He told me that he was sorry as well and if I ever want to play on any of his teams in the future just to let him know. Coach is also the coach of the high school baseball team and is one of the coaches on the track team. I believe he is also the coach of one of the really good softball teams that compete in the men's league in our town. As I walked home I regretted that I'd have to tell Sally that I could have been on the varsity basketball team, but decided not to. I felt she might be upset with me so I called her first thing when I got home. I had not told her about Coach's offer and I felt that I better get it out into the open quickly. I called her at about 4:00 p.m. and, although a little upset, she did not dwell on my decision. She told me that her parents want me to come over some evening and have supper with them. Although, considering my circumstance, I feel that I should have declined this offer; I did tell her that I would be glad to join them Friday evening for supper.

10/17/61

I did go to the Slater home tonight and arrived there at about 6:00 p.m. Sally was there at the doorway as I arrived and she looked beautiful. She quickly introduced me to her mom and her two younger sisters. Her dad had not yet arrived home from work and I was excited to meet him. In a few minutes her dad arrived and I was introduced to him. He is tall and I feel Sally looks like him more than her mother. I was glad that they didn't have a formal meal. They had just ordered a few pizzas from the local store and her dad had brought them home. We started to eat at the dining room table, but shortly Sally asked her parents if we could be excused and she and I took our pizza into the living room and finished it there. The television was turned on, but I cannot remember what was on for shows. Sally and I talked for about an hour and we did start a game of chess which we never completed. After a while her sisters came into the room and said they were going to bed. I smiled up at them and shook their hand and told them I should be headed home. As the two girls ran upstairs Sally and I went into the den where her parents were watching tv and I thanked them very much for inviting me over. They shook my hand and told me to come again. Sally showed me out and behind their front door gave me a quick kiss on my cheek. That was the first kiss that a girl ever gave to me. I will always remember this night because of that kiss.

10/20/61

I only saw Sally once today in the hallway at school. She was taking something out of her locker. I stopped for a minute and she asked me if I could walk her home after school. She said her parents had given the okay for her to do this. I told her that I'd be glad to. I told her that I'd meet her at the side door exit to the school at about 3:00 p.m. Sally showed up about 3:00 but asked if I'd mind waiting a few minutes for her as she had to talk to her English teacher. I had no problem with that and she went into the classroom to have her discussion. Just then I noticed Steve walking down the side driveway that leads to the rear of the school. I opened the exit door and asked him what he was doing. He told me he was going to give another look to the area around where we had located the pistol that night. I jokingly said to him that I was starting to think that he was making an effort to become our next sheriff. He laughed, but said that that was not a bad idea. He asked me if I wanted to join him and I told him I couldn't as I was going to walk Sally home. He smiled and continued walking to the back of the school. I started talking to a couple of my buddies for a minute and then Sally showed up and we left. Although it actually took us fifteen or twenty minutes to reach her house it seemed that it only took about five minutes and we got there far too quickly for my liking. I dropped her off and waved at her mom and sisters and headed home. I had gotten about halfway to my house and was confronted by Jerry Magee, one of the local town bullies. I had never had any dealings with Jerry, but that didn't stop him from grabbing me by my collar and humiliating me on the public sidewalk. The way I looked at it I only had two options. I could either stand there and take his abuse or I could hit him as hard as I could and hope that he'd then release me so that I could run home. Jerry is two or three years older than me and he weighs at least thirty pounds more than I do. Well, I decided that since he hadn't actually physically hurt me that I'd at least stand for this abuse for the time being. Just before I might have changed my mind and hit him, the sheriff pulled up beside us with his light flashing. I was very glad he showed up. Jerry was not as glad as I was when the sheriff grabbed him by his collar and pulled him away from me. I had seen fear before on occasion in people's eyes, but the fear that I saw today in Jerry's eyes I will never forget. While still holding the nincompoop by his collar the sheriff asked me if I wanted to have Jerry arrested. I thought for a moment and told the sheriff that it would not be necessary to do that. I told him that Jerry and I could handle the matter at a later time. The sheriff then pulled Jerry's face right up to his face and totally reamed him out in a fashion I had never heard before. He stated that he had heard of Jerry's bullying before and he never, never, never wanted to hear of it again. Jerry agreed to the max with the sheriff's order and stated that he would never do that again. The sheriff then turned Jerry around and pointed him down the sloped sidewalk and pushed him off abruptly and decisively. He then turned to me and asked if I was okay. I told him yes, thanks to him. He shook my hand and drove away. I truly believe that after seeing this unfold today that Jerry's bullying days are over. Nincompoop!!!

10/29/61

Nothing much noteworthy happened to me this week until today. Late this afternoon Steve called me and said he wanted to talk to me for a few minutes. I said okay to that and in about ten minutes he showed up driving one of the sheriff's department patrol cars. I ran out to see him as it was the first time I had seen him drive one of the cruisers. Steve told me to sit in with him as he wanted to talk. I jumped into the front seat and was enthralled with all of the equipment and weapons these cars have available. Steve didn't beat around the bush and stated that the reason he was there was to see if I had any interest in working in the sheriff's department. If I hadn't been seated snugly in the cruiser I probably would have fallen on my butt as this really took me off guard. He told me that he realized that I am not old enough to work for the department but stated that a brand new job was being created and what it is is to be an intern for the county on a part-time basis to help with the operation of the new communication system that had just been installed. The county commissioner had given approval for the hire and the intern would work about three hours per day four days per week. If hired he stated that I could work from 3:30 to 6:30 p.m. I asked him what made him think of me for the job. He told me that actually it was the sheriff's idea. He went on to say that Sheriff Dolloff knew that Steve and I were friends. He had asked Steve a bunch of questions about me apparently. Steve mentioned that Dolloff had been quite impressed with the way I handled myself the other day when I was confronted by bully Jerry. I thanked Steve and asked him to thank the sheriff as well and to tell him I would give him my decision the following day. I told Steve that I'd have to see if it was alright with my mom before I could give them an answer. I told him my grades at school have been good and I thought that I could keep them up and still work twelve hours per week. I hopped out of the cruiser and waved at my friend as he left. I went inside the house and sat down with Mom and she gave approval for my going to work as long as my grades did not suffer because of it. Tomorrow after school I will tell the sheriff that I'd love to work with him. As I close my eyes tonight in bed I realize that the only reason that I could possibly justify in my mind working with the local law enforcement department in town was because it would enable me to help Mom out financially.

10/30/61

I was excited all day at school because I was going to tell the powers to be in our county that I'd be glad to accept their offer and go to work for them. After school was out I went to the building that houses the police and sheriff's offices. I believe that I ran all the way from school to the building. I was winded as I arrived there and I asked if the sheriff was available. The sheriff wasn't there, but Steve was. He came out of the room that the deputies work out of with a smile on his face. He felt that I had decided to join them and I told him that he was right. Steve told me that the sheriff told him to tell me that I could start work next Monday. He said that he was very happy that I decided to come onboard and told me he'd be glad to introduce me to the police chief and the county commissioner if I'd like. I told him that would be great and he lead me down a long hallway that separates the two departments. As we walked he quietly mentioned to me that the position that I was taking was a great stepping stone to possibly becoming a full-time deputy in the future. I told him that had crossed my mind. Steve introduced me to Chief Jackson who surprised me in telling me that he is a distant relative of mine. He said that my mom is a very distant cousin of his. I shook his hand and told him that I was glad to meet him. I waved and smiled at those employees that were there in the office and then Steve took me upstairs to meet the commissioner. Commissioner Young is relatively new at his position having only been on the job for about one year. In fact, as I stepped into his office I realized that I have never even laid eyes on him before. He is quite tall and he shook my hand as I was introduced to him. He told me that he and his family had moved to town about two years ago and he had previously been commissioner for a county in northern Maine. He welcomed me and stated that the sheriff would be my boss. I thanked him again for the opportunity and shook his hand again before leaving his office. Steve then took me back to the ground level of the building and as I left I glanced back at the door that I just exited from. Steve was looking at me and gave me a thumbs-up sign and smiled at me. I can't wait until Monday, but I guess I will have to.

10/31/61

Halloween!! My sister, as usual, wanted me to walk around town with her for trick or treating. We left the house as dusk closed in and Mom stayed home to give treats out to the many kids that always came to our place. We saw many hobgoblins, ghouls and scary-faced creatures of the night during our travels, but we did receive a great abundance of candy and fruits of all sorts for our efforts. We did not try to scare anyone and did not mark up anyone's property on our trip. My sis was very cute and she was dressed as a princess and really looked the part. I carried two big shopping bags to hold our prizes and by about 8:00 p.m. we had pretty much filled both of the bags so we headed home. Mom told us that a few more than fifty kids had come to our door looking for treats and that they all had a good time. I snatched a few of my favorite candies to stash into my chest of drawers in my room and gave the rest of the candy and fruits to Mom to decide how to divide up. Sis gave me a big hug and went off to bed. Mom and I sat and watched television for a while and she told me that she feels that I am a great kid and a very fine brother to both of my siblings. She also stated she was proud that I am her son. Needless to say, I'm sure when the truth comes out showing what type person I really am a person's opinions about me will surely change.

11/4/61

Today, after school, I went directly to the sheriff's department to begin working at my first job. I was very excited! When I got there the sheriff was there and, first thing, he asked me to come into his office and told me to have a seat. He told me that today I'd be working with Joan Fraser who was also a recent hireling of the department and who had received a great deal of communication experience at another sheriff's office located in Pennsylvania. Sheriff Dolloff told me he had heard many good things about me and he was happy that I had joined the force. He then introduced me to Joan Fraser who took me to the area that we'd be working at. She seemed to be a very nice person and is quite young to have as much experience in this field as she does. She told deputy Perkins who had minded the switchboard for her that she'd resume her duties and he left to go on patrol. Joan wanted me to watch her activities today and at the end of my shift she said she'd ask me a few questions. I sat next to her and watched intently everything that she did. The job is a hectic one and there is much to know, just on the switchboard. Also, I'll need to know what types of calls I should take a message for and what type I should transfer to the proper recipient. The great thing about working in a busy atmosphere is that the time passes so quickly. Towards the end of my shift Joan asked me if I had any questions and I told her no. She then asked me what I had learned today. I thought for a moment and said that I had learned that this is a very important job and that it should be taken as such by every employee who works in the department. I said the job is hectic, but we should strive to be diplomatic, caring, efficient and thorough in all that we do. She then shook my hand and said that she felt my first day went well and that she would see me tomorrow. She stated that tomorrow I would be seated at the switchboard and will be training in the most important facet of my job.

11/5/61

Nervous, I guess I was nervous! I got to work a little early and I bought a cola to take with me to the switchboard. Joan was already there and jokingly told me not to get used to her being around this early in the day. She stated that she usually starts work at 4:00 p.m., but that she was going to come in early to work with me until they feel that I'm ready to solo on the board. She asked if I remembered the functions of the board. I stated that I felt fairly comfortable in my knowledge, but that we'd find out for sure over the next three hours. She stood up and wiped off the seat that she had been sitting in and made a motion with her arms beckoning me to the switchboard. I sat down and within ten seconds I received my very first call. All it was was a call to the sheriff and I transferred it into his office. The next call seemed urgent and I transferred it to deputy Oxton who was in his office. The deputy took the call and quickly left to follow up on a disturbance matter. He stated on the way out that he should be clear within twenty to thirty minutes. I logged that into our records and also logged that he was going to the Catholic church in town where someone was harassing the priest. Oxton arrived at the church in two minutes and found a homeless man there that had one too many adult beverages under his belt. He quickly invited the man to be seated into the back seat of his cruiser and drove him to the local homeless shelter. Oxton was clear and out on patrol in twenty-five minutes. The day went fairly smoothly for all of us in the department. At about 5:00 p.m. the sheriff tapped me on my shoulder and said he was going to the store and he offered to buy me a sandwich or something to eat. I declined his offer stating that Mom would be holding supper for me, but I thanked him very much for the offer. He told me that from what he had seen over the past two days that I was doing fine work and that I seemed to fit in with all of the staff. I walked home after my shift was over and felt very satisfied with that aspect of my life.

11/6/61

Something a little different happened in my life today. It was something I never had seen before and I hope that I will never see again. It happened not at home or at work, but strangely enough it happened in the first-floor men's room at the high school. It occurred after second period when I had ducked into the room to wash my hands. Our school has a circular fountain-type wash facility that operates by stepping onto the circular floor pedal when you wish to wash up. Numerous people can use it at any one time, but I was the only one there washing up. In the back of the room where the toilet stalls are located I could hear a commotion. Tom Wilbourn was at it again. He is another of our town bullies and he was picking on someone. I do not know who he was picking on, but I had heard him do this numerous times. Just then Jim Parker walked into the room. He saw that Tom was bullying and he grabbed him by his collar and dragged him into one of the stalls. I could hear Tom asking Jim to stop, but Jim did not stop. He lifted up the seat to the toilet and pushed Tom's face down into the filthy waters below. He then flushed the toilet several times with Tom's face still in the toilet. By this time the fellow that Tom was picking on had vacated the premises, not to be seen again. I quickly left the room also and went on to my next class. To my knowledge Jim could still be in that stall holding Tom's face where Jim surely felt that it belonged. I doubt if anyone will ever find out about this occurrence, but I will never forget it. Tom is a senior and he's a big tough farm boy, but he was no match for Jim. I'm sure Jim will never tell anyone about it as he'd get in trouble if he did. I'm sure Tom will never mention it as he'd be too ashamed to do so. The bullied kid will never mention it to anyone as he is ashamed of being bullied and is satisfied that Jim had taken care of business. Now I'm an employee of the sheriff's department and it is probably my duty to report what Jim had done. I am not going to, however. I dislike bullies with a passion and I feel that Jim had in his own way tried to teach Tom a lesson. I'm sure Tom will never forget this day. It is good to see the good in life overcome the evil and I have a feeling that Jim will be a stand-up type of individual for his entire life seeing to it that good wins out.

11/7/61

One of the very most enjoyable times in my life is when my sister and I are all alone in the morning. Mom heads for work really early as her shift starts at 5:00 a.m. I wake Sis up at about 6:00 a.m. and get some breakfast into her and make sure that she gets dressed. We both then make our own bed and then usually sit in front of the television watching her favorite cartoons for a few minutes before the school bus picks her up. Often she sits beside me on the couch and snuggles up to me. We usually only have about fifteen or twenty minutes each day to do this, but the love that we show for each other during these times is very special to me and I hope to her as well. I make sure she gets onto the bus all right and then I usually walk over to my school, weather permitting. In the winter months or if the weather is foul I will take the bus to school, but if it is nice out I enjoy the short walk to and from school and downtown to my job.

11/8/61

Sally didn't come to school today and I didn't have to work so when I got home I tried to call her. Her mom answered the phone and told me that Sally was quite sick and their doctor had made a house call and he felt that she had pneumonia. Mrs. Slater said that Sally had asked for me and was wondering if I could come over to their house for a quick visit. I told her that I'd be right over. When I arrived there Sally's mom showed me into the living room and Sally was laying on the couch in her pajamas and a robe. She looked very pale but her tired eyes sparkled as I came into the room. She was very happy to see me and reached out to me and held my hand. I asked her how she felt that she had gotten pneumonia and she truly had no idea how. Her mom sat in a chair with us in the room and we passed pleasantries. I felt Sally's forehead and it was hot. I handed her the glass of ginger ale that was sitting on the table next to the couch and she took a big drink. I told her that I hoped that she would feel better real soon and that I would pray for her recovery. As I left I gave her a wink of my eye and the thumbs up sign.

11/9/61

When my dad passed away my mom gave his rowboat to my brother. It has a small outboard motor on it and we usually go out fishing a few times each summer when he's in town. He told me I could take it out fishing any time I wanted to use it. Well, today I decided that I needed to get away for a while so I walked down to the mooring site and soon was headed out of the harbor. I veered to the northeast and traveled a mile or so out into Penobscot Bay and threw my hand line over the side of the boat. I had picked up a few clams at the fish market earlier this morning that I used for bait. I realized before heading out today that mackerel season is pretty well over and the chance of catching them this time of year is slim to none. It is very seldom that we get this nice of a day in November so I decided that I'd head out one more time this year before we store the boat for winter. I really didn't care if I caught any fish at all. I just needed to get away and do some thinking about my future. It was a gorgeous day and I looked in towards the beaches and surrounding areas that are part of my personal history. I was right; I didn't catch any mackerel. I did however catch a few nice flounders. I sat and did a lot of thinking. I also prayed that Sally would get better soon. I came to the conclusion that I could not live with myself if I didn't someday admit to the powers to be in town that I had made a great, great mistake. I prayed asking for God to please forgive me. My trip lasted just a little over three hours but I'm sure as time goes by I will consider it one of the most important events of my life. When I reached home I cut the flounders up and wrapped them up and took them to Sally's mom. I didn't speak to Sally as she was having a nap. I hope her mom will cook up a chowder tonight as it might help Sally in her recovery.

11/10/61

Today around 8:30 a.m. we were eating our breakfast and my brother drove into the driveway. We were not expecting him but it was sure good to see him. He asked me if I was available to help him to get the boat stored away for winter. I told him that I was and we drove down to the harbor shortly after brother Bob attached the boat trailer to his truck. It didn't take long for us to load the boat onto the trailer and get it home. Each year we put it into the back yard and cover it over with tarps. We take the outboard motor off and store it in the cellar. The most memorable part of this day was when Bob and I were down at the harbor and he told me that he was proud of me. I asked him why he was. He said that I was a very good brother and son to Mom and that I really was holding up my end of things in that I was the man of the house now. He stated that he felt I was doing a very good job with my school studies, was helping Mom with the family finances and was working at an honorable job at an early age. He also said that he was glad that I was there living with Mom and our sister to protect them if need be. When Dad died Mom gave me his two guns. The hunting rifle and .22 pistol are in my closet in my room. I thanked Bob for the praise and no more was said on that subject. When we got back to the house Bob sat with Mom and had a coffee before he headed home. My brother is a great guy and we sure miss his living locally where we could see him more often.

11/15/61

Nothing of importance has happened this week, until today. Sally came to school today and she is feeling much better. I spoke with her briefly after study hall and she told me that she had been very sick, but was now well on the mend. I told her I had missed seeing her, but felt it best to stay away from her for a few days and allow her plenty of time to rest and get feeling better. She told me that she had missed me as well. Although I would have liked to see her after school we decided it would be best for her to go home and rest. I told her that I'd call her tomorrow morning and if she felt up to it maybe we could get together for a while. As I close my diary tonight I marvel just how beautiful Sally is. She is not only beautiful to look at, but she is a very beautiful person inwardly as well. I am very lucky to have a meaningful friendship with her.

11/16/61

We got up around 8:00 a.m. today and had breakfast. Mom made pancakes and they were great. Around 9:00 a.m. I made a call over to Sally's house and she answered the phone. I told her that I'd like her to meet my family. I had discussed the possibility of her coming over to our place briefly this morning at the breakfast table and Mom said that it was okay with her. I told Sally that I could walk over to her house and we could walk together back to our place if her parents gave approval. She asked her mom if that would be okay and her mom said yes. I told Sally that I'd be over to see her in a few minutes. By the time that I arrived at her house Sally had bundled up in a beautiful new light blue winter coat and she also had on a ski cap. She told me that she realized that she was really overdressed as the weather was quite nice out, but her mom wanted her good and warm thinking only of Sally's health. Instead of walking directly to my house we decided to take a short walk through town first. We walked down Main St. and glanced into each store window as we passed. Some of the shops had already started with their decorations for Christmas, but most had their Thanksgiving decorations up. The town looked great and Sally did too. We went up Main St. taking in the beauty of the day and greeting all the people that we recognized. We then walked to my house. I was a little worried about Sally meeting my family but I need not have worried. Mom and my sister immediately took to liking her and Mom showed Sally the things that she and Sis were preparing to use as Christmas gifts this year. They were working at the breakfast table and Sally joined in and helped them for a while. Everyone was in good spirits and humor was abundant. Sally asked how my job was going at the sheriff's department and I told her that all seemed to be going well. After about an hour of wrapping various gifts Mom prepared soup and sandwiches for lunch. She felt the warm soup would be good for Sally and Sally agreed. At about 1:30 p.m. Sally told me that she should be heading home as she had told her mom that she'd be home no later than 2:00 p.m. She put on her coat and hat and gave Mom and Sis a hug. She told them that she was very glad to meet them and they said the same back to her. As we walked out the door Mom told Sally to come again and Sally said that she would. On the way back to the Slater's house I was almost in a trance. The day had gone so well and we were in such a good mood that almost without thinking I reached down and took Sally by the hand. Sally did not object and we walked hand in hand down the street. Next I did something that I had never done before. I asked Sally if she would be my girlfriend. I told her I knew other guys at school had asked her out and maybe that it was too soon to ask this question to her. She told me that she was glad that I had asked and that she'd be glad to go steady with me as my girlfriend. Before we got in eyesight of her house I gave her a little short kiss on her lips. I will remember that kiss and the smile she gave me for the rest of my life. Even more, I will remember her loving eyes that seemed to touch my soul.

11/20/61

The teachers at school told the junior class at the start of this school year that as far as preparing us for our future and going on to college, trade schools, prep schools or just finding a good job that this, the junior year, is the most important of our four high school years. It has, indeed, become that. What with working four days each week and trying to keep up with all of the homework that our teachers have been giving us I am exhausted by the end of my day. For the time being I will probably not post to this diary as much as I have been doing. I will try to at least enter comments about special events and happenings. Good night world. I'm dead tired!!

12/21/61

Today we had a staff meeting at work. It was the first such meeting that was held since I've been on the force. The whole staff except one patrol deputy attended. The sheriff updated us on recent news and then to my surprise he spoke of me. He stated that he felt that I had done an outstanding job and had fit in very well with all concerned. I think that I may have blushed a bit when everyone gave me a round of applause. The last thing that the sheriff said was that he had the honor to announce that Steve had been promoted and was now a sheriff's detective. We all gave him a big round of applause. Steve surely has earned it. After getting home I finished up a book report that I was working on. The report was on the book *My Life on The Plains* by General George Armstrong Custer. Before going to bed I called Sally and we spoke for about twenty minutes before I turned in for the night.

12/24/61

It took a little talking by Sally and I, but we were able to get both of our families to attend a Christmas Eve celebration at our church this evening. The families had not met prior to tonight so it was nice for us all to get together this way. We all sat in one pew and listened to three different choruses with piano accompaniment. The church was decorated beautifully and cookies, coffee, juices and cake were available. Sally and I had a big slice of the spice cake with great delight. As we left the church and after we had shaken hands with the pastor on the front steps I pulled a small wrapped present out of my coat pocket and handed it to Sally. She smiled at me and gave me a hug and kissed my cheek to the amusement of both families. I asked her to wait and to open it tomorrow morning, Christmas day. She said that she would and thanked me very much. She said that she hadn't brought the present she had for me this evening but would get it to me shortly. The families shook each other's hands and then we all went home. I sure hope that Sally likes the present that I gave her.

12/25/61

Sally called me this morning and she loved the present. It had taken quite a bit of thought for me to decide just what to give. I didn't have much money available and so I decided to give her something that I already owned. The present was a heart-shaped enamel cloisonne pin that had been given to me by my mother which she had inherited when her mom had passed away. I always loved this pin and it looks to be an antique but probably it isn't. All I know is that Gram had it in her jewelry box when she died. Sally told me that she had a present for me and would give it to me Monday at school. She told me that Santa had been good to her and that she received a ton of new clothes to wear. She had also received a year membership to the local YMCA from her parents. She told me she was going to try to get fit and lose some weight. I laughed at her and told her that she was already perfect in my eyes.

She made a point to really thank me so much for including the handwritten note that I had included as part of the gift I had given her. I can't remember all that I had written, but after she read it I'm sure that she knows exactly how I feel about her. I ended it with the words "I love you". That was the first time in my life that I had said that to anyone outside of my family. As Sally hung up she said to me boldly and without hesitation, "I love you too"!! I love Christmas and I love living in the beautiful state of Maine!!

12/30/61

At school today I saw Sally getting into her locker. She beckoned me to come see her. We were both in between classes so we just had a few moments to talk. She pulled a wrapped present out of the locker and handed it to me. She told me that she hoped that I would enjoy it and asked me to open it when I got home. I told her that I would and then the bell rang and we both headed off to our next class. I did not see her again today. I did work today, but it was kind of a non-descript and uneventful shift. When I reached home I opened the present. She had given me the top selling record album "West Side Story". I called her immediately and thanked her for this great gift. I told her that I had not played it yet as I had just gotten home from work. We talked for a few minutes and then she told me to go play the album as she had to go to dinner now. We hung up and I went upstairs and played it on my record player in my room. The album is great and I have a feeling that it might set all-time records for sales. I particularly enjoy the song "There's a Place for Us". I can't help thinking of Sally and I when I hear that song.

12/31/61

Tonight will be New Year's night. I had to work today but when I got home I asked if I could stay up tonight until midnight and ring in the new year with Sally, on the phone. Mom smiled and said that it was okay with her if it was okay with Sally's parents. I called Sally and brought up the idea and she liked it. I heard her ask her parents if that would be alright with them and they both said that it was, although not quite as easily as my mom had said so. Mom and sister, Terri, and I ate some pizza and watched television for a while and then they both went to bed about 9:00 p.m. Mom had let Terri stay up late to watch a scary movie on TV as there is no school tomorrow and she can sleep a little later. I watched a few New Year's Eve specials and then watched Jack Paar for a while before I called Sally at 11:50 p.m. She asked how my family was and I told her all was well. I could see the ball starting to come down on the building at Times Square in New York on the TV and I knew that a new year was now upon us. We didn't yell Happy New Year; we said it softly to each other at exactly the same time. I asked her if she knew how I feel about her and she definitely knew. We hung up at about 12:10. It was a good night.

4/30/62

I haven't written in this diary for some time, but I have a few minutes available tonight so I'll write a few words. School homework has been heavy, but I think that the worst of it is over now and we've completed most of the really important stuff that the teachers wanted to get through to us this year. Now, hopefully it will be downhill sledding for the remainder of the school year. Deputy Wells mentioned to us at work today something that had happened last night while he was cruising the county. At around 9:00 p.m. he was making his rounds and he was just coming over a rise on the road and a car zipped by him going in the other direction at a high rate of speed. Wells quickly pulled a U-turn and the chase was on. He followed the speeder for several miles but could not safely catch up to him. Just as he had decided to slow down and back off the speeder turned left onto a dirt road and turned off the headlights of the vehicle. Wells said he was lucky to see this as he almost continued by the road without seeing what the driver had done. Almost!! Wells turned onto the dirt road and soon found the vehicle that the driver had left on the side of the road. It had been turned off. He got out of his cruiser and checked out the car using a flashlight. Nobody was in it. All of a sudden he heard crashing sounds out in the woods. He quickly resumed the chase on foot through the woods. He kept getting closer and closer to the crashing and all of a sudden it stopped. He knew that he was close, very close, to the suspect. He turned off his flashlight and waited. And he waited and waited even more. After about twenty minutes Wells heard a man's voice yelling at him. The voice seemed to be coming from up in the sky! He flashed his light upward and what did he see but Vick Proctor climbing down from a tree stand. Proctor yelled out, "Boss don't shoot!! I've got to take a good healthy one, really bad!!" Wells chuckled and escorted Proctor out to the cruiser and handed him a roll of toilet paper he kept on hand to use in this type of emergency. He told him to go into the woods and do his business, but that he did not want to have to chase him again that night. Proctor disappeared for a few minutes into the bushes and then reappeared with head bent low. He had clearly been drinking and Wells let him know that he knew this. He told Vick that had he stopped earlier that all he would have received was a speeding ticket. But now, having tried to outrun the law which endangered everyone on the road, he was going to have to take him to jail to sober up. He told him that he hoped he had learned a lesson from this incident. He stated they'd leave it up to the judge who would see him in court the next day. Wells told us that we as law enforcement officers have to use everything available to us to apprehend suspects and in this case he had to use Proctor's bodily functions. We all laughed. Proctor spent the night in jail and the judge fined him $100 for his activities.

5/5/62

Today was a beautiful day! I had physical ed. class first period. Coach took us all out behind the gym and told us we'd be testing today. The first test was to throw a baseball. We all lined up and one by one threw a ball as far as we could down the playground. My first toss was the best in our class. Then came our second toss.

I threw my toss and then Will Collins threw one even further. He had thrown it at about a 45-degree angle. On our third and last toss I gave it my best effort and tossed the ball at about a 75-degree angle. The ball went and went and went. I believe it went about 310-320 feet or so. Collins tried to beat it, as all the other kids did as well, but my throw went the furthest. Then Coach said we were going to have a short race. The boys were divided up into a couple groups and Coach said that the heat that I was in looked to be a really fast one. Coach had driven a stake into the ground at the starting point and also down at the end of the playground. We were to go down and circle the far stake and return four times to complete the race. I had never raced competitively before and was racing against members of our track team. We took off fast, perhaps a little too fast, at least for me. I took the lead coming around the first stake and no one ever passed me. I was really tired at the end and I could hear some of the boys on the sideline yelling for Joe Kirkland who is a track team member to give a good effort as I was about to wear out. Well, he gave his effort, but he did not win and he wasn't really close to me at the end. I don't know how far we ran, but I finished in 2 minutes and 2 seconds. Later I heard that the only person to beat my time in the whole school was the local track star who ran a 2-minute time. I don't know how far we ran but that distance seemed to fit me well. Later I wished that I had run in the same heat as the local track star as it would have been interesting to see what might have happened. After that we rested for a few minutes and then went into the gym and we all did our standing broad jumps. We each had three tries. My best jump was 8 feet and 8 inches which I believe might be the best in the school. Then we did pull-ups to a metal bar. We had to do them correctly and I did 12 of them. We next did sit-ups and I did about 25 of them. The last thing we did, and it was the most difficult for me, was that we had to climb as high as we could up one of the ropes that hung from the gym ceiling. I am very afraid of heights but gave it a full effort and I was able to get to the top of the rope. After I had accomplished that I really didn't want to come down. I liked being up there and was glad to be away and by myself, at least for a minute or two. When I got home President Kennedy was speaking on the television and he was talking about Viet Nam. I didn't hear everything that he said but I sure hope that it does not escalate into a full-blown war over there. We have a few troops there already and I hope and pray that no more need to be sent.

5/9/62

I didn't feel good this morning but I went to school anyway. My grades have been good and I probably could go to college next year if we had any money in our family. Well, we don't, so that is pretty much that. I guess I'm leaning towards making law enforcement my life's work if the sheriff will promote me to a deputy when I graduate. Steve thinks that he will if there is a slot available, but I'm not sure how the sheriff feels on the subject. Sally has started working part-time at a retail store on Main Street. She is scheduled to work four hours Thursdays after school and four hours Saturday afternoons. The store deals in ladies clothing. I was glad that I didn't have to work today and went right home after school and now I'll turn in early. It is only 9:00 p.m. I still don't feel great. Maybe I'll be better tomorrow.

5/10/62

Brother Bob showed up today and we uncovered the boat and took it down to the harbor and moored it. We did start up the engine and took it out for a short spin around the bay. During the spin we got talking about Ted Williams. We both miss him very much now that he has retired. He is the only professional baseball player that I can truly say excited me each and every time he came up to bat. Well anyway, it is good to have the boat out and moored. The mackerel will be running soon. This was Sally's first official day at her job. I hope all went smoothly for her.

6/12/62

Today was our last day of school for the year. Sally and I are now seniors!! I will be doing a little painting with Mom on the back of our house this summer. Also, I plan to go fishing as much as possible. I heard that the mackerel have started to run so Mom, who loves to fish, and Sally and I will be going out onto the bay tomorrow to see if we can hit a school of them or two. This will be the first time Sally will go fishing with me. My aunt Barbara, my mom's sister, will take care of Terri while we are gone. She lives right in town and comes over to our place often. She loves Terri very much and enjoys their times together. The weather is supposed to be good tomorrow. I can't wait!!

6/13/62

I was up early today and anxious to get started. Aunt Barbara picked up Sally at her house on her way over to take care of Terri today. She also drove the three of us down to the harbor and dropped us off. We were in the boat and headed out onto Penobscot Bay by 8:15 a.m. I headed up the coast in a northerly direction. Mom took it upon herself to rig the hand lines that we'd be using. She was good at it after much practice over the years. She rigged three hand lines for us and each one she set up with three hooks which set about three feet apart on the lines. We travelled for almost a half hour and I decided to drop anchor off a point of land that stuck out into the bay. Man did we hit them!! I never have gotten into a school of mackerel like that before. We were pulling them in hand over fist for close to two hours. Several times we were able to land three fish with one drop of the line. When things started to slow down a bit I counted the fish that we had caught. There were 49 mackerel sitting on the floor of the boat. I figured that was enough for one day's catch and by 11:30 a.m. we were back and moored the boat. I called Aunt Barb at the house and told her we were back and asked if she'd pick us up. I asked her to please bring some aluminum foil and large plastic bags so that we could wrap our catch up and keep it clean and fresh. We hadn't kept count of how many fish each of us caught but Mom, I'm sure, caught the most. I bet she caught at least 50% of the total catch. We got home and set to cleaning the fish. We cut them up and wrapped them in foil with four or five fish being in each wrapped pack. Mom and I kept two packs and we gave two packs to Sally to take home and the rest we gave to our neighbors to enjoy. It was really a wonderful day today.

6/19/62

Today at work it started out quietly but that didn't last long. Just before 4:00 p.m. we received a call from a lady who seemed out of breath and very upset. She stated that she had just witnessed a large moving van roll over and fall down an embankment in front of her house. She stated she lived three miles out of town on Route 1. I told her I would have help to them immediately. First I called the fire department and then I called the state police. Next I called the nearest sheriff's department cruiser to the accident. Then I called the local ambulance service. Each of my calls emphasized the need for immediate responses. It took me six minutes to make these calls. The fire department was the first to have a unit there. The van had crashed through the guardrail and rolled down a steep 25-foot embankment. The driver was still in the cab of the truck but he seemed to be unconscious. There was blood on the windows of the vehicle. At approximately the same time two state police cars and our department's cruiser arrived and these men walked the road north and south of the accident to direct traffic. The ambulance arrived and waited nearby until they were needed. Deputy Wells arrived on the scene and he helped wherever he could and kept me informed as to what was happening as best he could. The man in the truck was conscious now and I heard him yell a couple of times. He was in a great deal of pain. Well, it took several hours to get the man out of the truck as the cab had collapsed around his body. As I got off duty at 6:30 p.m. Deputy Walker was heading up to the accident site and he asked if I wanted to come along. I jumped into his cruiser and we went to the site. We arrived just in time to help lift the man on a stretcher up the steep embankment and into the ambulance. The man was still alive and he didn't appear to have any broken bones. The only injury that I noticed was a gash he had that went from the top of his head to his chin. It was bleeding quite badly, but the paramedics were working on that area. The driver was communicating by this time and stated that he had apparently fallen asleep while driving. Several wreckers had shown up and they were pulling the van up and onto the highway. In a way it was good that the van's windshield had broken as it made it a lot easier for the paramedics to reach and work on the accident victim. He will probably carry that scar for the rest of his life on his face but at least he will live to tell about it.

6/24/62

One of the nicest things that happens to me on an ongoing basis happens on work days as I leave our house. I start walking downhill on the walkway in front of the house and I look upward to our front window. In it, almost always, is Terri and Mom and they are waving and smiling at me. It makes me feel good to receive such a sendoff and it brings me to the realization that they will be there when I get home and will be there always for me as they love me. The most important thing that happened at work today is that Sheriff Dolloff announced to us that he would be retiring towards the end of next year. He stated he hadn't decided an exact date yet but he'd let us know soon what his decision will be. He said that next year he will be sixty-seven years old and after working in the department for forty years it will be time to let fresh blood take over the leadership of the department. We will all miss him, I'm sure, as will the entire county. I have a feeling that possibly a couple of the staff will throw their hat into the ring and campaign to be our next sheriff.

6/28/62

Today something happened to me that I have a feeling I will never get over. Brother Bob joined Mom, Uncle Ben (Barbara's husband), and I and we started to refurbish our house. Mom and Terri did some touch-up painting on the back of the house and the three boys re-shingled the front of our roof. Bob and Ben did all the hammering as they both have some talent as carpenters. I climbed the long ladder and kept the boys' supply of shingles and nails and tools available to them. We had the radio playing while we worked and one of the songs that played made me think of Sally. The song was "Portrait of My Love" by Steve Lawrence. It is a beautiful song and I can't help but think of her when I hear it. There is an old saying that "I almost bought the farm today" that people sometimes use when they almost die in an accident. The thought I guess is if someone dies they might have life insurance and this insurance once cashed in will allow the deceased's family to pay off their mortgage. I guess that's what the quote means. By the way Mom does have a small life insurance policy on Terri and me. She dropped the one she had on Bob when he went out on his own. Well, about 10:30 a.m. I brought an armful of shingles up to the boys. It was quite hot so I climbed onto the roof to rest a bit before I went back down the ladder. Our house is pretty high and they were working on the right side of it. Our tarred driveway is on the right side of the house. I was wearing my sneakers and squatting down looking out over the side towards the driveway. All of a sudden for some reason my sneakers kind of slipped and I was going downhill on the roof which has quite a slant to it. I only slipped about six inches, but if I had slipped any more I would have fallen approximately twenty-five feet onto the tarred driveway. I believe God was with me today and I really don't know how I prevented going off of the roof. My tread on my sneakers is almost gone as they are old and once you start sliding on a steep surface it is very hard, almost impossible, to stop sliding. Our job was not complete until about 8:00 p.m. tonight and I, for one, was glad that it was done. I didn't climb up onto the roof again after

34

my near mishap and to tell the truth I will never again climb up a long ladder or get onto a roof of any kind in my life. I was very afraid today! I did not like heights before today and now they scare me to death. I have a feeling that I'll have nightmares of this event for the rest of my life. Truly today I almost bought the farm!!

7/4/62

Sally and I thought it was time for our two families to get together again so we decided to meet for ice cream at the soda shop at 8:00 p.m. and then go over to the city park to enjoy the fireworks display celebrating the holiday. We all arrived on time and Sally's dad picked up the tab for all of us. After much good conversation and ice cream we walked over to the park and awaited the fireworks. It was a beautiful night and Terri was having fun with several of her schoolmates that were there also. The rest of us sat on the lawn on blankets that we brought along. Sally and I sat alone on one blanket and Mom and Sally's family sat on another blanket. The conversation was great and then it started. The whole sky lit up with fireworks in front of us and out into the river! The rumble of them echoing off the distant shore brought me to thinking of how battles must have sounded in years now gone by. The crew putting on the show really outdid themselves tonight. I have seen many holiday fireworks displays, but this one was by far the best. Well, just maybe, I feel it was the best because Sally was sitting next to me snuggling my arm and enjoying our time together. Far too soon the final heavy round of fireworks went off and we all went home. Both of Sally's parents made a point to tell me it was great to see me again before we split up and went home. A good time was had by all. Mom and Mr. and Mrs. Slater seem to be becoming friends.

7/11/62

Today was pretty much an uneventful day at work. When I got home Aunt Barbara's car was in the driveway. I went into the house and Auntie and Mom were sitting on the couch in the living room. Mom had her robe on and her feet were soaking in a small plastic tub. I asked what was going on and she told me she had taken a spill at work today. She always soft sells her injuries and physical problems so I asked to see her bruise if she had one. She had her pajamas on already and pulled up the back of her pajama top to let me see. She has a very bad bruise on her lower back which is about the size of a softball. It's red and purplish and it looks to be very sore. Also, she has a smaller bruise on the back of her neck. Apparently, what had happened was that she was lifting some large boxes from the ground floor at the mill and was bringing them up onto the second floor and she had tripped on the stairs. She fell backwards and it shook her up pretty badly. Thankfully it happened at the end of the day and one of her co-workers drove her home. I asked her if she felt better now and she said that she'd be ready to go back to work on Monday. I'm glad this is Friday and she'll have a couple of days to heal and get feeling better. I asked her if she wanted to go to the hospital or to see a doctor and she said no to that.

7/14/62

Mom did go back to work today. I wish that she didn't, but she did. She is a very tough individual and she has a steadfast work ethic. When there is work to be done at the mill she is always the first to pitch in and always the last to leave when it is done. After my work tonight Sheriff Dolloff saw that I was leaving and he asked me into his office. Just then deputy Wells walked past the Sheriff's office and let out an earth-shaking belch!! Everyone in the department got a good chuckle out of that and then the sheriff hollered out to him, "Bring it up again and we'll put it up for a vote." By that time everyone in the department was in stitches. Wells smiled and jokingly stuck up his middle finger at everyone in general. The sheriff then asked me to close the door so we could talk privately. He was still chuckling. He told me that Wells' gesture put him to thinking about something that had happened many years ago. He said that everything he was about to say to me was to be just between the two of us. I assured him that it would be so. He stated that years ago he had a friend that was the manager of the local finance company. His friend worked late one evening to close a loan to a fisherman that could only come in to sign papers after 7:00 p.m. The long line crew member fished out of New Bedford but he was home after a recent catch. The man apparently signed the papers and then asked for the manager to give him the loan disbursement in cash. That was okay with the manager and he counted out $2000 and gave it to the man. Then the man stepped out onto Main Street and looked back into the finance office and right into the eyes of the manager. The fisherman smiled and stuck up his middle finger at the manager who instantly realized that he had made a bad mistake in making this loan and that the man had no intentions to ever repay it. Sheriff Dolloff got wind of his friend's problem and decided to go speak to the fisherman the next evening at the man's apartment. Dolloff arrived around 5:30 p.m. and made a point to walk heavily and menacingly up the long stairway that led up to the man's rent. He banged on the door which was opened quickly and it was plain to see and to smell that the fisherman had partaken of at least a few adult beverages. Dolloff didn't sit down and he quickly told the man that he knew of the rude gesture that he had pointed in the direction of the manager last night. He told him in no uncertain terms that he would strongly recommend that he make each and every payment for the duration of that loan on time or ahead of time. He told him if he didn't do this that he, the sheriff, would take it upon himself to make sure that he'd regret not doing so. The sheriff is a large man and in his uniform I'm sure he looked very intimidating to the inebriated idiot that was now seated at his kitchen table looking up at him. Dolloff told me that this is all that occurred that night and that he just walked out of the door slamming it behind him. Dolloff was now chuckling again and he told me that the outcome of this story was that the fisherman went into the finance company the next day and paid the whole loan off. I laughed at this. He told me that the reason he was telling me this was not to try to teach me to be any certain way but just to show me that things are not always black and white and often they can be gray. He said that most assuredly he stepped over the line on this matter and could have gotten into a lot of trouble. He was very happy with the outcome however and the finance company manager never found out what had happened that evening. Dolloff said that we, as law enforcement officers over the years make many friends and many enemies. He went on to say that most of us that take up this kind of work have it in common that we like good to prevail over bad. That is why he stuck his neck out that night and did what he felt was right. Before I left his office he reiterated that if I wanted to become a deputy after high school graduation that he would do what he could to see that this occurred. He stated that he'd be a short-timer by my graduation day and that the new sheriff would be elected in November of next year but that he'd help me in any way that he could. I left his office tonight thinking of him not only as being our sheriff and boss, but also as him being my friend.

8/1/62

I haven't had much time to write in my diary lately but I'll write a few words now. I've been thinking about what the sheriff said about my future plans. I guess I've pretty much decided that I'd like to work in the sheriff's department but one thing that I do know is that I do not want to work full time in lock up. The people who work day after day in the jail have a very rough job. I realize if I become a deputy and go out on patrol that there will be times that I'll have to muckle onto drunks and people trying to escape and forcefully bring them into lockup. I know that, but deputies also do a lot of positive things in the community and help people in many ways daily. You have to be very cautious if you are a turnkey. They have to always remember to be vigilant. They should remember that no pens or pencils should be allowed in the cells. Inmates have killed law enforcement officers with sharp objects like pencils. I have a small amount of pity for anyone that gets thrown into one of our 19 cells. For 23 hours each day they are there in their cell and the monotony must be close to unbearable. One hour each day they can go outside and get a breath of fresh air. They are enclosed in an exercise area with dimensions of 30' x 25' which is surrounded by very high fencing. Barbed wire is also included as a deterrent at the top of the fence. Over the years our department has been lucky in that we only had one person commit suicide while incarcerated. That happened many years ago and lockup now is a very systematic and vigilant area. Most of the really bad criminals are not with us for long. They go before our judge and are quickly moved to the prison in Thomaston to serve their sentence. If all that is available next year for a job in this department is a lockup job I will pass. I do not want a job there. However, I would be very interested in becoming a patrol deputy.

8/14/62

At 4:45 p.m. today I was at the switchboard and received a call from one of the officers down at our local bank. The man sounded upset so I put him through directly to Sheriff Dolloff. I could hear the sheriff in his office and he stated to the banker that he'd be right over to see him. The sheriff left abruptly and didn't return until about 6:00 p.m. He did call in once at 5:15 p.m. saying that he'd be going to see Bill Madison out at his house near the lake and he'd be back at the office soon. When he returned he told Steve and I what all the fuss was about. Apparently, the bank vice-president had turned down a loan request that had been requested by Madison. The request was for $100,000 which was a far greater amount than any previous request that the man had made. He was a long-time bank customer and he was very mad that the request was denied as he had always paid each of his accounts in a timely fashion. Well, Madison apparently blew up and lost his temper and swore loudly at everyone in general as he left the bank and he alluded to the fact that the vice-president's chair was quite visible to people on the street and it would be terrible if anything ever came through his window and hit him. The banker was quite anxious and he took the comment as a threat. He stayed out of his office until the sheriff had arrived as he knew Madison had a very bad temper and he just might do something foolish. Dolloff went to Madison's residence and found him there. He still was very upset and irritable but the sheriff sat down with him and had a cup of coffee and by the time he left the house Madison had calmed down and apologized for the incident. Dolloff let the man know that he could have been arrested for the threat to the banker but stated that the bank did not want to pursue that as long as the matter is now closed and that there would be no further problem from him. Madison assured Dolloff that the matter was now closed.

9/2/62

Alan Clewley is somewhat of a legend at our school. He is a very funny guy. Well, today he really did outdo his past accomplishments. I was on hand and saw bits and pieces of it. Don't ask me how I know it was him that did it; I just know Al. Somehow he had gotten into Principal Runcy's office and had absconded with his golf pants, shirt, hat and shoes. He was aware that Runcy liked to play golf after school these beautiful summer days. Al apparently did this at the end of the day and he, or someone working with him, had raised the garments to the top of the flagpole in front of our school. As we all left for the day we could hear Runcy's epithets clearly as he located the whereabouts of his garments. Al smiled and winked at me as we vacated the premises. Yes, the legend of Al grew even greater today. This was our first day back to school for the year.

9/7/62

Brother Bob showed up today and we went out fishing for a short time this morning. We only caught four mackerel, but we did catch five nice flounder. He left early in the afternoon as he had another engagement this evening. Before Bob left he went out to his truck and brought a record album into the house. He said,

"Here, this is yours. I enjoyed it and I hope you like it as much as I do." The album is Harry Belafonte's "Return To Carnegie Hall" album. Although it had been released a couple of years ago I had not heard any of the songs on it. I thanked Bob very much and he left after giving Mom and Terri a kiss. After supper I went upstairs to my room and played the record. I listened to it very carefully and really liked it. The song that caught my ear the most is "I Know Where I'm Going". It brought me to thinking about Sally and helped me to realize that she is very important to me. Her happiness must be a strong factor in how I proceed in life. I think that I'd like to marry her someday but realize that my wish more than likely will never materialize. Around 8:00 p.m. I called Sally and talked with her for a while. After running out of things to say to her I told her that I wanted to play a song to her that I really love. She said that was okay and I played the Belafonte song to her. After it was over she whispered, "I love you, Billy", into the phone. I could hear that she was very emotional and that she was crying. I whispered back to her, "I love you too." She then said goodnight to me and hung up. Part of me thought that I should call her back to see if she was alright. However, I decided not to call back. I am sure that after she heard the song that she truly knows that she'll rest forever in my heart.

9/10/62

I got quite a surprise at work today. The sheriff asked if I'd like to join him tomorrow at an event that was to be held at 1:00 p.m. at the high school. The fire chief and a few of his firefighters were going to say a few words about fire prevention and the sheriff was asked to make a few comments about drugs and driver safety. He said I'd be there at school anyway and the kids would really like to see me in my new sheriff's department shirt. I told him I didn't have a sheriff's department shirt. He opened up the bottom drawer in his desk and pulled out a white package and tossed it to me. He smiled at me and said, "Well, you do now!" I opened it up immediately and tried it on. It fit me perfectly. Needless to say, I was very happy and, yes, proud. I told him I'd be glad to join him at the event. He asked me to give some thought tonight so that I would be able to say a few words about driver safety tomorrow. I told him that I would. Mom and Terri were delighted to see my new shirt when I got home.

9/11/62

Wow!! Today was a great day. I, for one, will never forget it. I didn't tell anyone that I'd be speaking at the all-school event. I didn't even tell Sally. At 1:00 p.m. we all left our classrooms and walked down to the gymnasium. I kind of lagged behind and ducked into the men's room before entering the gym. I told the sheriff that I'd meet him there and would put on my new shirt. The sheriff was there already and asked me if I was prepared to say a few words. I told him that I was. The fire chief and his firefighters were the first to speak. They gave about a twenty-minute presentation. Dolloff told me he wanted to go next and said I should stay in the men's room until he announced me. Surprisingly I was not really nervous. I had given a lot of thought last night to what I would say and I felt comfortable that it would turn out alright. All the students and all the teachers were seated on the gym bleachers. Mr. Runcy, our principal, was at the microphone on the gym floor and he was announcing who would be speaking next. The sheriff is well liked in our county and he received a nice round of applause as he walked into the gym and up to the mic. He spoke for about fifteen minutes and concentrated pretty much on the illicit drug problem. Then he whispered into Mr. Runcy's ear asking him to come and get me at the men's room. He did come to get me and in a few seconds I was entering the gym as Sheriff Dolloff introduced me as being the newest member of the sheriff's department and who is one of your own, Bill Todd!! I couldn't believe the reception that I received!! They gave me a standing ovation!! I walked up to the mic and Dolloff and Mr. Runcy stood behind me as I spoke. I did see Sally in the crowd and she waved at me. I spoke for about ten minutes and it went well and I hit upon most of the points that I wanted to. As I was closing I stated that when you are tired while driving to remember to stop and get out of your vehicle and get a breath of fresh air and do not continue your journey until you are fully awake and responsive. I mentioned the trucker's accident out on Route 1 and stated if he had gotten out of the truck and taken a short break perhaps he never would have wrecked that day. Just then the sheriff walked to my side and nodded to me indicating that he'd like to say something. I backed off the mic and Dolloff said, "I don't know if any of you know it, but Bill helped out a great deal the day that this wreck occurred. He was at the switchboard and made sure all emergency personnel got to the accident site quickly. He also went to the site, although he was off duty at the time, and was one of the men that lifted the accident victim up over a 25- or 30-foot embankment and into a waiting ambulance." Again, everyone in the bleachers rose to their feet and gave the sheriff and I a thunderous round of applause as we left the gym. As we walked out of the door Dolloff looked at me and gave me a wink and a smile and said, "Well that went well, didn't it?" I truly cannot believe what happened today and I'm very proud of the outcome.

9/13/62

Today is my birthday. I'm seventeen and it has been a most enjoyable day. Sally asked me what I wanted for a birthday gift from her and I asked her to take me out for a pizza and then take me to a movie. She did just that, tonight. The pizza was my favorite, hamburg, mushrooms and onions and we ate at the pizza shop in town. I walked over to Sally's and then we went to the pizza shop. After eating we walked up to the theatre, picked up a large buttered popcorn bag and went in and watched *The Man Who Shot Liberty Valance*. We enjoyed it very much. Afterwards I walked Sally home and I got home about 9:30 p.m. Mom was still awake and wished me a happy birthday and gave me a big hug and said that I'd have to wait until tomorrow to receive my gift from her and Terri. I have absolutely no clue what they might have gotten me.

9/14/62

WOW!! I still can't believe what happened today!! We were eating breakfast at about 9:00 a.m. and brother Bob came through the door. I wasn't expecting him. He had a big smile on his face. Mom came up to me and told me my present was out in front of the house. I ran to the living room and looked out and I couldn't see anything on the lawn. Mom, Bob and Terri laughed at that and Mom told me to look out a little further, closer to the road. All I could see was a car that was parked there. Mom nodded and told me yes, that it was mine. They all hugged me and wished me a very Happy Birthday. I ran outside and jumped into the driver's seat. The car is a 1958 Ford Custom 300. It is blue and white and it only has 12,554 miles on it. The family had gathered around the car and I asked Mom how she was able to afford it. She told me she had sold Dad's car and the proceeds plus money that Bob and Terri had put in was plenty enough to buy it. The car is beautiful!! I took driver's ed when I was fifteen years old and already have my license. I never thought that I'd be able to have a car, at least not until I had full-time work. Mom said I could keep it in the garage at night as there is plenty of room in there now. They all hugged me again and then Bob asked me to drive him down to the bus stop as he was going to go home by bus. He said he had plans for this afternoon so he better leave now and catch the early bus home. I drove Bob downtown to the bus stop and waited with him until it arrived. I thanked him again and gave him another hug as he stepped onto the bus. I waved at him until he was out of sight. Needless to say, this being Saturday, I took a quick spin over to Sally's on the way home. She was incredulous when she saw the car. I didn't stay long as they had company, but Sally and her family liked the car very much. I realize that I drove illegally today as I haven't registered the car yet or got plates on it, but I will take care of that before I go out on the road again. We can't have a sheriff's office employee get in trouble on a driving infraction now can we?

9/27/62

I got a call from brother Bob this evening and we decided to take one last trip out into the bay tomorrow to see if we can catch a few fish. After that we plan to bring the boat home and stow it away for the season. We only got out fishing a few times this year as it has been pretty busy for all of us.

9/28/62

Bob showed up a little after 9:00 a.m. and we drove down to the harbor after picking up a few clams at the fish market. We've always had good luck using clams for bait. Terri went with us today as Mom and Sally both had to work. She had been out in the boat several times before, but this was the first time that she was going to try to catch a fish. Usually when we go out onto Penobscot Bay fishing we head north but this time we decided to head southeast toward the Atlantic Ocean. As usual we used hand lines. We never have gotten into using poles like most fishermen do. I guess it's kind of a family thing. My dad always fished with hand lines as his father did before him. We travelled about a mile out and then started fishing. Terri was very excited and expectant. After about ten minutes I got a good bite and pulled in a nice-sized flounder. Terri was all eyes and her excitement grew. Bob was next to get a bite and he pulled in another flounder. Just as he was taking his fish off the hook Terri got her first bite. We had told her once you get a bite to jerk your line so that the hook will set firmly. She remembered and, after a very exciting fight, the fish was pulled aboard with Bob's help. It was the biggest one yet and Terri was very happy and proud to have landed it. We fished for a couple of hours and caught six flounder and two mackerel. Afterwards we brought the boat home and stowed it away for the winter behind our house. Before he left Bob noticed that I had gotten my car registered and licensed. I told him that I plan to put it up for the winter towards the end of October so that it will stay in good shape and not be adversely affected by the ice and snow and salt on our Maine roads. He felt that was a good idea. I told him I'd keep the car in the garage safe and sound and that I only had a short way to walk to get to school and also to get to my job. Bob reminded me to check the oil level in the car and to wash and wax it when I put it up for winter. Terri caught three fish and, I'm sure, will always remember today.

10/13/62

I didn't get much sleep last night and I'm exhausted today. I layed there in bed and could not stop thinking and worrying about the biggest mistake of my life. I got so upset that I almost literally got physically sick to my stomach. I guess most people who have broken the law and have not been caught would try to forget what they've done and move on with their lives. But, I was not raised that way. I was brought up to know right is right and wrong is wrong and if we do wrong we should own up to what we've done and try to make it right if we can. As time passes I feel more and more each day that someday I will have to admit my grave error. I hope I sleep better tonight.

12/2/62

I haven't written in my diary lately, but I will now. I have been quite busy of late and today was kind of a slow day so I have a few minutes to write. I know this will sound strange, but I've come to believe that I just might be gifted with extra sensory perception. One example of this occurred tonight. I stopped over to the YMCA after work and hoped to shoot a few games of pool at the tables before going home. Both tables were being used so I sat on a bench and watched. Monte Martinez was practicing on one of the tables and instead of asking him to have a game I thought that I'd be better served in watching him. He is a very good player. He didn't mind me watching him as we are already friends. He's in the army and is home on leave currently. After watching him for about half an hour I stood up to leave and Monte said goodnight to me. Without thinking I blurted out, "Monte, your mother is a nurse, right?" He said, "Yes." I added, "And your father is deceased, right?" He said, "Yes, but how did you know that? We've never discussed them before; how did you know that?" I just looked at him and said, "Monte, I don't know." This is just one such occurrence that has happened to me over the years. I feel that it is possible that I could be a little psychic. That worries me as lately I have felt that I will have to own up to my terrible mistake sometime in the next year or possibly what I did will be found out by a party or parties. I have not been sleeping well lately.

12/25/62

We had a great time today. Mom asked Sally and her family over to our house for our noon meal. She baked a really nice ham, cooked potatoes and sweet potatoes as well as squash, and all and all it was a really nice meal. For my Christmas presents Mom had bought me another sheriff's department shirt that she had ordered with the help of the sheriff, two pair of khaki pants that I can wear as part of my uniform and several record albums. Santa was good, as always, to all of us and he had left a brand new bike for Terri under our tree. The Slaters brought to Mom a big box of chocolates, a big can of cashew nuts and a bottle of wine. Terri, Bob and I chipped in and bought Mom a really warm winter coat. Her old one is getting pretty seedy after years of use. Bob showed up just before lunch and enjoyed the day with us. I bought a really pretty blouse and gave it to Sally and she gave me a warm winter sweater which I quickly pulled on to the delight of all. The Slaters left around 4:00 p.m. as did Bob. Mom, Terri and I spent the rest of the day lounging around and watching TV. I went upstairs after supper and played my new albums. Very enjoyable day!!

1/2/63

Yesterday was New Year's Day and it was pretty much uneventful for the Todd family. I did speak to Sally on the phone and we did wish each other a Happy New Year at midnight. That was two nights ago. At work today we got the news of who will be running for the office of sheriff. Sheriff Dolloff will be retiring at the end of the year and three candidates announced today that they will be running for the office. Deputy Wells who has been with the department for years is running as a Democrat. And Thatcher Rodman who used to be a New York City sergeant on the police force is also running as a Democrat. To my surprise Steve Morrissey announced that he would be running for the office as a Republican. I thought it quite unusual that Steve would jump in and run as he hasn't been with the force very long. I also think that it is great that he is running and by his doing this he will bring some excitement and a new face to the campaign. I have a feeling that he just might do really well as he is a great communicator both in front of an audience and with everyday people on the streets. No one apparently will be opposing Steve as a Republican, but Wells and Rodman will have to have a runoff in June to see who will be on the ballot as a Democrat. Although I would really like to see Steve win the election I will not openly talk of this as I want to remain seemingly impartial to everyone's eyes on this matter. I'm sure Sheriff Dolloff will not openly back any of the candidates for the same reason. I truly do not know who Dolloff would favor for the position.

1/13/63

I spoke briefly with the sheriff today and he told me about something that had happened to Steve last night on his shift. Steve was on a stakeout trying to gather information and evidence on a drug deal and he had just left his location and was driving back to the sheriff's office when he spotted something out of the corner of his eye. It was snowing and there was already about three or

48

four inches of new snow on the ground but he noticed a car parked in the alley beside the local pub. It looked to have one, possibly two, flat tires so he pulled over to take a better look. It was icy and very slippery as he walked down the alleyway. He brushed some of the snow off the side windows as he reached the vehicle. It looked to be an abandoned auto. Steve went to the other side of the car and to his amazement a man was laying there passed out in the snow. Steve quickly checked the man's vitals and found out that he was barely breathing. It was very cold last night and at the time it was about 10 below zero with a wind chill of nearly 20 below. Steve quickly tried a mouth to mouth procedure on the man and he seemed to start breathing a little better. Next he picked the man up in his arms and walked up the steep, slippery alleyway and got him into the warm pub. He laid him in the back office of the bar and told the owner to call an ambulance immediately. The man reeked of booze and probably was very drunk. Steve had no idea how long the man had been laying there so he asked the bar manager if this fellow had been into his establishment and, if so, when he had left. He was told that the man had been drinking there about a half hour ago and then had purchased a round of drinks for the few patrons that were there and had left. Just then the ambulance arrived and the man was quickly transported to the emergency room at the hospital. Steve, although he was at that time over with his shift, followed the ambulance to the hospital and stayed there until the doctor came out to the waiting room and told him that the man was suffering from frostbite but that he was now cognizant and was communicative. Steve then left and checked in at the office and then left for the day. The sheriff told me what the drunk's name is but I can't remember it as I write this down tonight. I do know that Steve most assuredly saved this fellow's life and I have a pretty good idea who the man will be voting for in the upcoming election. The sheriff knows the man and has asked him to come to his office when he is able to. Dolloff will make the decision whether to charge the man with public drunkenness or not. He might very well give him a pass this time as the man surely suffered and hopefully has learned a good lesson. Dolloff also told me that he'd be making a little visit to see the owner of the bar as he would like to get an answer to why this man was allowed to drink so much at his establishment that he ended up almost losing his life. If Dolloff doesn't get what he feels to be satisfactory answers he will probably have to report the incident to our state offices in Augusta for them to follow up on.

1/29/63

I was talking to Sally tonight on the phone and blurted out something that I probably shouldn't have. It was surely not planned, but I slipped and said something to the order of, maybe we'll marry one day. Sally did not hesitate with her response and said, "I would like that." I was upstairs in Mom's room using her phone and Sally was upstairs at her house. We talked for quite a while and I told her that I did not plan to go on to college after graduating this year from high school. I told her that I have a pretty good chance to be hired full-time by the sheriff's department after graduating and that I like that type of work very much so I'm planning on giving that possibility a try. Sally has very good grades in school and I believe her parents want her to continue with her education. She has even better grades than I have. She told me that when it came to deciding what her future would be that she felt that her parents would more than likely go along with whatever she decided to do as long as she would be happy with that decision. She told me that her employer was very happy with her work and that she had told Sally already that if she wanted a full-time position after graduation that there would be one for her there at the store. I am falling deeper and deeper in love with her as each day passes. I realize that we are both very young and there is a world of negatives working against us. The biggest negative is whether or not I'll be able to live with myself as a human being if I don't own up to the one great mistake of my life. I might very well be doing Sally a great favor if I break off our relationship now before it develops even further. I have a lot to decide and I pray each night for the guidance to move on in a proper path. I probably would come clean right now if it wasn't for my mom. She has been hurt enough in her life and I cannot bear to see her hurt again. I will not allow her to be hurt again.

2/13/63

I got to work this afternoon and was told that there had been an armed robbery today at a branch office of a bank in Gorham. There were believed to be two white men involved and they were to be considered armed and dangerous. They were both carrying pistols and were last seen driving a large and long black car which appeared to have out of state plates on it. The men had taken an undisclosed amount of money and drove away from the branch in a northerly direction at about 3:00 p.m. Our dispatch department had just gotten word of this so we called out to all of our cruisers and made the deputies aware to be on the lookout for this type of vehicle. It was thought that the men just might make a run and try to cross Maine's border and get into Canada to make their escape. Steve was on duty and he had pulled over onto a dirt road off Route 1 and was eyeing the traffic that passed on the main route. He had a couple of apples and was chewing on them at 5:31 p.m. when I received a call from his unit. He sounded excited and said he had just seen a large black car with out-of-state plates heading north on Route 1 at a pretty high rate of speed. He had started the pursuit and was closing the distance between his cruiser and the black auto. I told him to be very careful. He said he was going to try to pull the vehicle over and that there were no other vehicles to be seen at that time. The next five minutes were perhaps the longest five minutes I have ever experienced. Nothing was heard from Steve during those minutes. The other dispatcher and I made sure that all of our department's cruisers were aware what was happening and to be ready to respond quickly if need be. I asked one of the deputies that was only about two minutes away from Steve to head over there quickly just in case. We also made the state police aware of what was going on and they had several units in the area that would respond immediately. We heard nothing from Steve for at least five minutes and then, finally, he responded and he sounded out of breath and excited. He said that he had been shot on his right foot but it wasn't a bad injury. He said he was trying to keep sight of the fleeing car which was headed north at a high rate of speed. Steve said that he had fired two shots at the car as it sped away. He suggested that all possible units should set up a barricade of sorts at the three-corner intersection in Prospect as quickly as possible. Dispatch made the needed calls and we were in hope that the units would arrive there in time. Those units did arrive in Prospect in time and as the black car approached the intersection it stopped about 600 feet from the barricade. It pulled a quick U-turn on the road and headed in a southerly direction. Steve had stopped on the road and was now about a quarter of a mile in front of the suspect's vehicle. Behind Steve was a state police cruiser that was speeding to join him to close the door on our unwanted guests. The state cruiser did join Steve and they set up a barricade using both of their vehicles. It didn't take long for an outcome and there was never a stand-off. The driver of the black car stepped out of his car with his hands high in the air and dropped to the cold dark pavement as Steve and the state police officer handcuffed him. I had dispatched emergency medical units to the sight as I thought they might be needed. They quickly got Steve into a unit and bandaged up the foot that had been hit by the gunman's bullet. What had apparently happened in the five minutes that we hadn't heard from Steve was that he had pulled the black car over and he had parked beside the road about 60 feet behind the black vehicle. Steve had gotten out of his cruiser and was standing behind his car door and he yelled for the passengers to turn off their vehicle and step out of it and onto the road. The suspect on the passenger side of the vehicle stepped out and he had his hands in his coat pockets. Steve told the man to show him his hands and the man pulled out a pistol very quickly and touched off two shots in Steve's direction. It was very dark and cold, but Steve felt the first round glance off Route 1 and slice into the side of his right shoe. The shot tore down the side of the shoe and also grazed the side of Steve's foot. The second shot Steve heard whiz by his right ear. The man quickly jumped into the black auto which sped away. As it was pulling away Steve fired two shots at the back of the vehicle. He then got back into his unit and called dispatch and resumed the pursuit of the black car. What we all found out later was that the man on the passenger side of the vehicle was dead and apparently one of Steve's shots had hit him on the head. Sheriff Dolloff had been right behind me observing this whole event and he felt that it had gone very well all in all. The sheriff wanted the emergency unit to take Steve to the hospital and said that he'd be up there before the unit arrived. He wanted to check to see how Steve was doing. I was now off duty, but I asked Dolloff if I could go with him to the hospital. He told me to jump into SD unit #1 and we went to the emergency department over at the hospital. It wasn't long after we arrived at the ER that the unit carrying Steve arrived. He seemed to be in good shape medically and was bandaged up and also seemed to be okay mentally even though he knew that he had just more than likely ended the life of a man. We were all very thankful that we had made it through this very eventful day.

2/14/63

Sheriff Dolloff asked Steve to make out a full report of yesterday's events. He told him that he would be put on leave for perhaps as much as two weeks and in that time the county and state officials would investigate the shooting of the suspect thoroughly to determine if Steve, indeed, did shoot the man and if the shooting was justified. Dolloff told Steve that this was just standard procedure and that he felt that Steve had nothing to worry about. Steve completed his written report and left it with the sheriff. Dolloff also spoke to Steve for about an hour behind closed doors and asked him any questions that he had after reading the report. Steve left the department at about 11:00 a.m. and most of the staff shook his hand as he left. I was not at the department when all this occurred but received word of it when I came on duty. Dolloff asked Steve to leave his pistol with him as it would be needed in the investigation and Steve had done this.

2/25/63

The news was released today that Steve's actions on the night of 2/13 had been a "good shoot" and he had been cleared of any wrongdoing. It had been determined that it was his pistol which when fired had killed the suspect. He had shot at a fleeing, gun toting, man that had just shot two times at him. One of those rounds had hit him on his foot. Both suspects had been previously described as armed and dangerous. He had reason to believe that the suspects were fleeing bank robbers. Dolloff called Steve early this morning and he came in to work shortly thereafter. We were all very glad to have him back with us. Upon arriving at work today I was asked by Dolloff to join Joan Fraser and him in his office. Dolloff asked us both just to kind of keep an eye on Steve to see that he is acting as his old self over the next few days. He stated that the shooting might begin to bother Steve at some point so we should be watchful to assure he is alright. Dolloff stated that he feels Steve is okay and we'll probably not notice any difference in him at all. None of us in the department will ever mention that night to Steve again unless he, himself, brings up the subject.

3/10/63

Everything seems back to normal in my life not only at work, but at school as well. Steve is doing fine. There has been a lot of talk throughout the county as to who people favor to be our next sheriff but I don't feel there is much difference currently in the way people are leaning. If there isn't a major gaffe made by one of the candidates I feel it will be a pretty close election. Mom came home from work early today which is very uncharacteristic of her. She said that she was slightly nauseous and had some back pain. When I got home from work I told her that I felt she should take tomorrow off and go in to see our doctor. She told me that she thought she'd be fine by tomorrow and that she might have picked up a touch of the flu bug that was going around. I agreed that it might be the flu, but why did she feel she had back pain? She told me not to worry about it and that it would be fine tomorrow. Mom is very stubborn and does not miss work unless she absolutely has to. I did talk her into going to bed early this evening so hopefully things will be better with her tomorrow.

3/14/63

I don't know!! I am quite upset with Mom at this point. She did go back to work on Tuesday, the day after she came home from work early because she was sick. She was no longer nauseous, but I could tell that something was still bothering her by the way she walked. She has been working ever since that day. She did tell me last night that she still has pain in her back. I will keep a close eye on her and if things don't improve I will have the doctor come to our house to see her if she refuses to go see him. On a positive note, things are great between Sally and I. We are becoming closer and closer each day in our relationship. I love her very much!!

3/21/63

I don't keep up on daily happenings in the news as much as I probably should. I think I did hear recently that Patsy Cline had died in a plane crash. If so, that is very sad as she, in my opinion, is the greatest female country singer of all time. I did hear on the nightly news tonight that Attorney General Bobby Kennedy closed down the Alcatraz Federal Prison for good today. That place sure has seen its share of infamous people over the years. Mom seems to be doing a little better lately. I am glad that her friend, Hazel, is kind enough to pick her up at our door each morning and get her to work. They have worked together for years and are good friends. Hazel also drops Mom off after work when Mom doesn't feel like walking home. Lately she has not felt up to the walk.

3/26/63

I got home after work today and grabbed a sandwich and went upstairs to my room. I was laying on my bed and had just started to do my homework when Terri came into the room. She looked very tired and yawned as she climbed up onto the bed beside me. She watched me reading from my school book for a few minutes and then laid her head down on my pillow and snuggled up to me. Within a minute she was sound asleep. I continued my homework and about a half hour later when done with it I picked Terri up and brought her to her room and got her shoes off and tucked her in for the night. At eight years old I feel she is doing very well in life considering she has lost her dad at such a young age. She is very smart and has an outgoing humorous nature. People seem to like her very much once they get to know her. Mom did mention to me this evening that her longtime workmate, Ted "Leaky Boots" Alexander, had passed away in his sleep last night. He had been still working at the mill at age 71 and he was the employee that had worked there the longest according to Mom. He had picked up the nickname "Leaky Boots" as he was an avid fisherman and he always wore the same old leaky boots year after year when he went out to fish. He could have afforded to purchase new boots, but he was kind of superstitious in that he felt if he changed boots that his luck in fishing might change as well. He was over the years known to be a very successful fisherman. Ted was believed to be an alcoholic and he was known to indulge in adult beverages after work each evening. Most people also felt that he had a bottle tucked away somewhere at the mill that he'd nip on occasion. He was Mom's friend and she was saddened by his passing. I met him a few times over the years and liked him as well. He was almost always the last person to leave the mill at the end of the day and he usually locked up all the doors and made sure all the windows were down and latched. It crossed my mind that with his passing a very possible witness to some of the happenings that occurred on the night of 9/7/61 was now gone and would never have to testify in any court of law.

4/1/63

April Fools' Day!! Of course there were the usual pranks today at work for April Fools. Mom got me with one early this morning before she left for work. She hollered upstairs to me to get dressed quickly as she wanted me to run up to the local convenience store and get some milk as she needed it to bake something with. I quickly got dressed and ran downstairs and she and Terri were waiting at the bottom of the stairs smiling ear to ear. They both yelled out, "April Fool" and I realized that I had been had, once again. She gets me every year and I don't know how she does it. Dolloff and Joan Fraser got deputy Wells pretty good today. Joan called out to Wells asking him to respond to a fisticuffs situation at our local restaurant. He responded and arrived at the eatery about a minute after receiving Joan's dispatch. What he found as he hurried through the front door was Dolloff with a big smile on his face and he heard those annual words, "April Fool!!" The sheriff made nice though and bought Wells lunch.

4/12/63

Saturday, so I had the day off from work and school today. I decided I'd take my car to the local service station and get an oil change and grease job done. Terri came with me and we got home about 10:00 a.m. I got the hose out and a bucket and started to give her a once-over wash. Needless to say, Terri came out and wanted to help me. I prepared a second bucket for her and she did a pretty good job on the areas of the auto that she could reach. I told her that I'd take her to the ice-cream parlor later for a treat for helping me out. We did that, with Mom's approval, after supper. We had a nice time today together. We don't get much time to do things alone together and it was a treat to be with her today. School and my job and Sally and my homework take up most of my time. Terri is very well liked by everyone that she meets. I hope and pray that life will be kind to her.

5/3/63

Today was quite busy for a Saturday. Bob had called last night and we agreed that we should put the boat out. He arrived around 9:00 a.m. and we went out for a short excursion up the coast and were back to moor the boat by 11:30. It was beautiful out on the bay today. We did not fish at all, but agreed that we'd have to soon when the mackerel start running. Bob ate lunch with us and then headed home. I laid down for a short nap and then called Sally on the phone. I told her the drive-in movie was opening for the season tonight and wondered if she wanted to go with me to see Alfred Hitchcock's *The Birds*. She sounded like she'd really like to go with me, but said that she'd have to discuss it with her parents first. She said she'd hang up and call me back shortly after she talks to them. About fifteen minutes later the phone rang and she asked if I could come over to their place around 4:00 p.m. as her parents wanted to talk to me. I told her I'd be there around 4:00. Well, at 4:00 when I got there Mr. and Mrs. Slater and Sally were in their living room and Mr. Slater greeted me at the door and asked me to join them. I could tell by his uneasiness that Mr. Slater was hunting for the right words to say, so I thought that I'd beat him to it and say a few words. I told them that I am a very safe driver and that I keep my speed well below the speed limit at all times. I told them to fear not as Sally has already informed me in no uncertain terms that any adult ideas that I might have kicking around in my head will have to wait until man's law and God's law would approve of them. Everyone laughed when I said that and Mr. Slater quickly gave approval for us to go out tonight and he shook my hand. We left a few minutes later and we went to the sandwich shop for a bite to eat before movie time. My car was all shined up and she liked it very much. We saw a couple of the high school kids at the shop and hung around with them as we ate. When we finished we drove down to the shore and got out of the car and walked along the beach until dusk approached. We then drove down to the drive-in and got our popcorn and sodas before the movie started. My feeling is that a movie just isn't a movie unless you have a big bag of buttered popcorn to munch on. Well, we had a ball and the movie was really good. I had heard someone say that Hitchcock feels that this is his most scary movie so far. I think Sally would agree with that as she snuggled with me for most of the movie. We did indulge in a number of kisses and I noticed that most of them happened after a scary scene had occurred. All in all, it was a great night and I got Sally home well before the deadline that Mr. Slater had given me to get her home by. Mom and Terri had gone to bed by the time I got home but Mom heard my steps as I walked upstairs and she called me into her room and gave me a hug and asked me how it went tonight. I told her that all went well and that we had a great time. She smiled and I went to bed.

5/8/63

He was a simple man. He was strong, but kind. He worked every day of his adult life and tried his best to support his family. I've played a lot of baseball and softball in my life, but the most memorable baseball happening that ever occurred to me was the one time that he had a catch with me. He never competed in sports, at least not in my lifetime. He never had time for competing in such activities as he was always working. He did like watching sports on TV however. The only time I can ever remember seeing him cry is when he had to have an operation on a hernia. He had to take a few days off from work as the doctor had ordered. I was quite young at the time and Dad was in the living room resting. I walked in to see him and he was crying. I didn't know what to do so I went into the kitchen and told Mom that he was crying. She thought I must be mistaken and went in to check for herself and found that yes, he was crying. She consoled him and gave him a hug and asked what was wrong. Well, what it all boiled down to is that he hated not being able to work and support the family. This upset him very much. I will remember the catch I had with him that day forever. He was very smart and had a good sense of humor. He taught me many lessons. I hope that eventually I'll be as good of a man as he was. I miss him very much. Today is my Dad's birthday. Happy Birthday Dad!! I miss you!!

5/17/63

Brother Bob came up this morning and we went out fishing for the first time this season. It's kind of early in the year and the mackerel have not started to run yet. We love going out onto the Penobscot Bay and Penobscot River. When we are out there we are away from all of the hum drum daily nuisances that seem to clog our minds occasionally. We can point our boat in any direction that we wish and leave our daily troubles behind us for a few short and wonderful hours. Bob told me to keep an eye on Mom as he felt she hasn't been acting like she is in the best of health lately. I told him that she seems to walk differently now and she doesn't seem to have the old vim and vigor like she used to. Just then Bob got a good strike on his hand line. All it was was a good-sized dog fish. He quickly pulled the hook out of the fish's mouth and released it back into the bay to live another day. As we travelled up the coast I could see familiar homes, ones that I had mowed lawns at when I was younger. Many memories came back to me as we progressed to the north, all of them good memories. We fished for about three hours and then returned and moored our boat. Our day's catch consisted of six dog fish, which we released, and five flounder that we cooked up for supper tonight before Bob headed home. It was a very enjoyable day.

5/23/63

I got a big surprise today. I was off duty as it's Friday, but Steve called me and told me that deputy Rodman had announced today that he was dropping out of the race to become our next sheriff. To the press he just stated that he was doing it for personal reasons. However, off the record, he told Dolloff and Steve that his campaign had not taken off as he thought it would and he really didn't have enough time to dedicate to a truly active race. He felt the odds, considering he was from out of state and would be trying to beat two local boys, were slim. I congratulated Steve and told him one down and one to go. Deputy Steeves will be the Democrat on the ballot in November. I have a feeling that it will be a pretty close election as both Steve and Steeves are well liked and are very competent at their jobs. At school today we, the senior class, practiced marching for our upcoming graduation. In a short time Sally and I will be out in the work force, hopefully with full-time jobs.

5/28/63

When I got to work today Sheriff Dolloff asked me to join him in his office. He told me that Joan Fraser had put in a two-week notice and she would be leaving the department. She had been contacted by the sheriff in her hometown and he offered her the same job as she has now down there. It is a much bigger department and her salary would be larger and, again, it is her hometown so she accepted his offer. Joan told us that she didn't make her decision easily as she loves mid-coast Maine and likes all of the people in our department very much. It was just too good of an offer for her to turn down. Dolloff told me that when she leaves he'd like me to take over as department head of the communications department. I didn't have to think long and I told him that I'd be proud to. He added that he realizes that eventually that I would like to become a deputy and go out on patrol and he felt this move would be the right move for me to make in pointing to that goal. Joan joined us for a minute and shook my hand and congratulated me on my upcoming promotion as a full-time employee. Mom and Terri were very excited to receive the news tonight when I got home.

6/7/63

Graduation, I felt, was kind of anticlimactic. For twelve years we work hard on our studies and then we are done. Some of our class will go on to college and probably Sally and I could join them, but I never really liked school all that much. I will not go on in my schooling and I don't think Sally intends to go on either. It was a beautiful day and the graduation was held outside on the football field. Tonight our class had two graduation parties, as I guess most graduation classes do. One party was held at the local dance hall and was attended by about half of the class. The other party I heard occurred down on a sandy beach just north of town. It was rumored that adult beverages would be available at the beach party. Sally and I decided to make an appearance for a short time at the dance party. We felt that if we attended the beach party everyone would probably vacate the area when I, a sheriff's department employee, came upon the scene. We stayed and danced for about an hour and then left. We went to my house for a while and talked to Mom. Terri was already in bed. Mom said she really liked the speech that Caroline Taylor made at graduation. Caroline is an ex-movie star and she is very well liked by everyone in our community. The main gist of the speech emphasized that we should have fun and enjoy our lives. She recommended that we find jobs that we enjoy doing, ones that almost don't feel like work. She stated if we are lucky enough to find that type of employment we'll be the happier for it. She said that only about 5% of people ever find that type of a job. 95% work for their whole careers at jobs that they really dislike. Afterwards I drove Sally home and dropped her off. We are both now free to make our way through life as best we can. It has been a long day and a long twelve years.

6/14/63

Terri, Mom and I went out fishing today. We had heard that the mackerel were just starting to run so we thought we'd give it a try. By 9:00 a.m. we were loaded up and had purchased a few clams at the fish market to use for bait and were headed out of the harbor. This time we headed in a southerly direction. My thought was if the fish are now running they are coming into the bay and up the Penobscot River from south to north so I felt our chances might increase by heading south. Both Mom and Terri were very excited. We travelled for a mile or so down the coast and dropped anchor. It didn't take long for Mom to bait Terri's hook for her and also to get hers baited and out into the bay. Bang, Mom got a bite within the first minute that her line was overboard! It was a good-sized mackerel and the fun began. Terri and I got bites next and we both got our fish onboard. We fished for perhaps two hours and caught four flounders and twenty-four mackerel. We decided to head back home as the sun was high and hot in the sky and Terri was getting close to being seasick. The rocking of the boat did not agree with her, at least not today. I will always remember this day of fishing with two of my three lady loves. Mom was vibrant and active and so was Terri. We told Terri some of the old family stories that are passed from one generation to another here on the Penobscot. She listened intently and took it all in. On the way home we stopped by the Slaters' and left half of our catch with Mr. Slater. He was very happy to receive our gift. One of the stories we told Terri today was one that my grandmother had told me. She had said that in years gone by Penobscot River had totally frozen over one winter all the way from Lincolnville to Islesboro. I can't remember if she told me she had seen that happen or that it happened before her time. Needless to say it had to have been really cold for a long duration for that to ever have happened. She told me that people went out onto the ice and walked all the way to Islesboro from Lincolnville.

6/20/63

Joan Fraser stopped by the department today on the way out of town. She was headed to her hometown and will start work at the sheriff's department there next week. I thanked her for all the help she had given me in learning my trade. She told me that it had been an easy task to teach me as I was a natural at our type of work. She visited each of the staff that were there and also made a few calls out to the guys in the cruisers and said her goodbyes. I asked her to keep in touch with us but I realize when one door closes another opens and usually once someone leaves an area most if not all ties are cut. She will be missed. Dolloff called me into his office for a few minutes. He told me that I should be proud of myself being head of my department at the age of seventeen. He said there was a lot of serious responsibility that goes with my job and that he feels very confident that I can handle it. He added if he didn't feel that way that I would not have received the promotion that I had. As I was leaving his office I asked if he'd like to join me in going fishing sometime. He said that he would like that and stated maybe later in the season we could get together. I told him to let me know when he is ready. We ate some of the mackerel that we had caught the other day when I got home tonight. I actually get home earlier now than when I was working part-time. Now I'm usually home by 5:30 pm and before I usually didn't get home until about 7:00 p.m.

7/1/63

Something happened to me today that, now that it's over, I can't really fathom that it truly occurred. I got out of work as usual and was driving home and I decided to stop and pick up a gallon of milk. I walked into the store and made my purchase then walked out of the store and started across the parking lot to get to my car. Just before I reached my car I saw a young lady step out of her vehicle and she walked toward me as if she was heading into the store. I recognized that she was one of my classmates and I said "Hi" to her. She walked up to me and slapped my face, hard!! I was incredulous, but the instinct for self-preservation came over me and I slapped her back, just not nearly as hard as she had done to me. I asked her why she had done that and she just continued to walk and the last I saw of her she had entered the store. I hardly even know the girl and have not talked to her much over the years. As far as I know we have never argued or had ill feelings towards one another. Why then did Margie Fredericks slap me as she did? I guess I could have her arrested if I wanted to, but I guess I'll just file it away under the heading "Nuts I've Dealt With In My Life".

7/3/63

I received a nice surprise today. Dolloff asked me into his office and asked if I wanted to join him tomorrow in the parade up in Brooks which celebrates the holiday. He said that the town officials had contacted him and invited him to make an appearance. He said we could take one of the cruisers and I could drive the unit and we'd do some waving and candy throwing and it should be fun. I told him I'd love to join him. He said if I wanted to have Sally join us that would be fine. He told me to juggle my staff's schedules so that I would not have to work tomorrow. He said that he'd pick us up around 9:00 a.m. as the parade starts at 10:00. I hope we have nice weather tomorrow. I have attended their 4th. of July event several times in the past and, considering it is a very small town, they usually get a large crowd to watch the parade and contests as well as the fireworks that they shoot off after dark. Also, they usually have several music groups that play during the day. I called Sally and she said she'd love to go with us. She is still working only part-time, but has accepted a full-time job at the shop starting in early December to help prepare them for the Christmas rush. Sally does not have to work tomorrow.

7/4/63

Dolloff picked me up today at 8:45a.m. and we stopped at our local store and picked up three large coffees to go and a bag full of doughnuts. We then picked up Sally and headed up to Brooks. Sally looked very pretty and she had her hair in a ponytail. She sat in the front seat of the cruiser between Dolloff and I. Sally and the sheriff didn't know each other very well so they introduced themselves to each other and did most of the talking on the way. We arrived in Brooks at about 9:45 and the participants who would be in the parade were already lining up. One of the parade officials came over to our cruiser and asked if the sheriff would lead off the parade and be the first in line. He said that he'd be glad to and opened his door and beckoned me over to do the driving. He had brought a large paper bag in which he had lots of candies for us to throw to the kids along the parade route. At 10:00 a.m. sharp a pistol was shot and the parade began. I drove very slowly so that we would not get ahead of the rest of the folks behind us. There were several marching bands among the entrants and their music was lively and patriotic. Sally kept Dolloff and I supplied with candy and we threw it out to the people who had gathered. The day was beautiful and there was a very large crowd gathered. We saw many people that we know along the route. All three of us were in very good humor and we had a ball today. Dolloff and I tried to relax and just have fun, but we are both law enforcement officials and sometimes it's hard to not see what is right in front of you. I saw a minimum of a half-dozen unregistered vehicles up there today and mentioned it to Dolloff as we headed home. He said, "I saw more than that, but they can wait. If we did anything today about those infractions we'd destroy any goodwill that we had built this day. We'll let the boys handle those infractions piecemeal over the next month or so. Country people are a little different than city people; they have to be shown over a period of time what is expected of them. They are good old boys and they mean well, but they need to be nudged at times to get them to walk down the straight and narrow." Dolloff concluded his thought by saying, "We'll get all of those vehicles registered; it will just take a little time to do it."

7/19/63

Well, Dolloff and I finally got together and went out fishing today. Unlike my family, he uses a rod when he fishes. The Todds have always used hand lines even way back beyond all of our memories. Dolloff was in rare form and really enjoyed himself today. He is a very personable person and he can be very funny at times. We left the mooring at 8:30 a.m. The sheriff told me that he has enjoyed his job very much over the years, but he is glad that his time is winding down now and he looks forward to his retirement. He said he just might buy a boat similar to ours and do some fishing and might get a membership at the golf course if he can find his old clubs. I had heard that the mackerel were running really hard right now and we were both really excited to see if that was the case. We headed north, up the bay, and stayed pretty close to land. We travelled for about a half hour and then dropped anchor just off a point of land that I had fished off many times before. Bang!! It didn't take long!! We were hitting them left and right. I had my line rigged so that I had three hooks on it at different levels and, at one point, I caught three mackerel on one cast. Dolloff was having a great time and was hauling them in to beat the band. We caught a few flounder and far too many dogfish. We threw all the dogfish back so that they could be a nuisance again on another day. Dolloff was lucky and caught a striped bass. Actually, he was very lucky as I have never been fortunate enough to catch one. We also caught thirty-nine mackerel and five flounder for our day's work. We divided up the fish equally between us and I gave half of my share to Mr. Slater on the way home. I told Dolloff that I hoped we could go out again before season's end and he agreed with that idea. I enjoyed my time with him today.

8/2/63

I had a big surprise today. This morning Mr. Slater called me on the phone. He told me he and his family were taking a vacation and they'd be heading to Florida shortly. He wanted to know if I could get time off from work and be able to join them. He stated it would be his treat and they'd love to have me come along. I thanked him very much and asked if I could give it some thought and I would call him back in a few minutes. He said that was fine. I went up to my room and sat on my bed, but I guess I really knew all along that I wouldn't be able to go with them. I knew that Sally would be really disappointed, but knew that my decision was the correct one. There were two major reasons that I decided against going and both would be kept as my secret forever. First, and most importantly, I felt that I shouldn't leave my mom at this time. I just have a gut feeling that her health is not as good as she'd like us to believe it is. I would not feel right about going off and leaving her at this time. Secondly, I must admit that since the time that I nearly fell off our roof while we were shingling I have been deathly afraid of heights. They will be flying to Florida and I don't think that I'll ever fly again. I did fly once when I was eight years old. Dad took me up in a small single prop plane at a local fair just to get a view of the area. Dad did not pilot the plane. We went up as the pilot was selling thirty-minute flights to all that wanted to get a bird's-eye view of mid-coast Maine. I was pretty afraid back then and can only imagine how I'd feel now were I to fly again. I called Mr. Slater back and told him I would not be able to join them, but I was truly honored by his invitation.

8/11/63

Well, Sally and her family left for Florida today. They flew out of the Rockland Airport in a small twin engine plane. I followed their car down to the airport and Sally rode with me in my car. She was sad that I was not going with them. I just told her it didn't work out this time, but hopefully someday we'll be able to vacation together. All of the female Slaters were really excited as none of them had ever flown before. I helped Mr. Slater carry the baggage into the terminal. Their flight took off at 12:03 p.m. I could see Sally clearly looking out at me from one of the windows located toward the rear of the plane. She was waving at me and I'm sure her family was as well, but I never saw them at all as my eyes were fixed upon Sally's smile. They will be gone for about a week. I will miss her very much. They were flying to Boston and then they'd get onto a larger plane for the flight down to Florida. I will pray that all goes well for them and that they have no mishaps on their trip.

8/15/63

I had just gotten to work this morning and I sat down at my switchboard and I received what appeared to be an urgent call. It sounded to be a relatively young boy on the line. He sounded out of breath and he yelled into his phone that there had been a bomb planted at the grade school in town. He told me to come quick as the bomb would go off in an hour. Then his phone cleared and he was no longer on the line. I felt that it was probably a false report, but just in case I quickly called the town police chief and told him what had happened and also called the fire chief with this information. Within ten minutes five police officers and a fire truck arrived at the school. I had called the principal at the school directly after calling the police chief and fire chief and told him that we'd advise that the school be evacuated immediately. The principal sounded quite perturbed and he stated that this had happened previously, about a month ago. I called in to Sheriff Dolloff and made him aware of what was going on. He thought for a minute and then asked one of the deputies to check the records at the school as to who had called in sick today and also on the day that the last bomb threat had occurred. In about twenty minutes this information was brought to Dolloff. He quickly left in a cruiser and said that he'd be on a stakeout for a while on lower Allyn St. About an hour and a half after he left he returned but made no comment as to what he had done. Later, at the end of the day, he asked me to come into his office and close the door behind me. I did and he told me to sit down. He stated that what he was going to tell me was off the record and he wanted it to stay between the two of us only. I assured him that it would. He told me that after he had looked at the attendance records for the grade school for both days in which bomb scares had occurred he thought it might pay to go and have a discussion with Robby Norwood, one of the students. Robby had been absent both days and he was known to be a wild and troubled kid at times. Dolloff said that Robby lives on Allyn St. and so he took an unmarked cruiser down and staked out at the lower end of Allyn just below where Robby lives. He waited for about a half hour and then saw Robby run down the sloped street and into his house. He continued to watch the house and about ten minutes later Robby came out and started to walk up the street. Dolloff got out of his vehicle and called the kid over to him. He asked him where he was going. Robby apparently seemed confused but stated he was going to the convenience store. The sheriff asked him what he was going to buy and he said milk. He volunteered that he had been up to the store earlier to get milk but decided to get some more. Dolloff asked the boy to take him into the house. Robby said nobody was home, but it was okay to come in. Dolloff asked Robby to show him the milk container that he had purchased earlier that day. Robby opened the refrigerator and showed Dolloff a nearly empty gallon of milk. He laughed and said, "Rob, you must really like milk!" Robby said that it was really hot today and that he does really love milk. Dolloff then asked him what he was doing home today as it was a school day. Rob said he was sick. The sheriff then mentioned that Robby had been absent another day not too long ago. The boy said that he had been ill that day too. The sheriff told Rob that he didn't want to see him get into trouble and that truancy is a serious matter. He recommended that the boy get into his pajamas and get into bed. He stated that's where sick people should be and he asked if Rob agreed. Rob did agree. He went on to tell Robby that both days that he had been out sick there had been bomb scares called into his school. He asked the boy if he was aware of that and Robby said no. The sheriff had been sitting on the couch in the living room and he then stood up and told the kid to get feeling well real soon. He opened the front door and just before he departed he turned and looked at the kid and said, "You know that telephone companies keep very accurate records of what calls are made from each individual phone, right Robby?" He answered that he did know that. Dolloff then left and told the kid to have a nice day. I smiled at the sheriff and told him that I thought we might have a dramatic decrease in the number of bomb scares in the future. I had found out earlier in the day that the police and fire department personnel had thoroughly searched the school and no bomb had been found. The students were allowed to go back to their classes at 10:45 a.m. They had been playing out on the school playground for the duration of the search.

8/21/63

Not much happened of note today, but I did talk with Steve briefly as we ate our brown bag lunches at work. He told me that early next month he would start to get active in his campaigning to become our next sheriff. He told me if he has one regret in his work so far in the department it is that he has not been able to solve the Rance Edwards homicide case. He told me that he had solved every other case that had been assigned to him but not that one. He told me he felt the election was going to be a very close one and if he could solve that case it just might be enough to push him over the top and get him elected. That was all that was said as just then there was a call and Steve had to leave quickly in response to a family dispute out in the county.

9/3/63

I was sitting in the lunchroom at work today eating and Deputy Wells and Steve were also there eating. They both agreed that they were not going to spend a lot of money on their campaigns. They said they'd probably put up a few signs in key locations. They agreed not to debate, but Steve said that he had a friend who is a disc jockey at the local radio station and he had brought up the idea of both candidates coming onto the air at drive time and just making a short statement live as to what they feel are the key issues facing the county currently in law enforcement. Steve thought that was a good idea and asked Wells what he thought. Wells considered the idea for a few minutes and said it was fine with him and for Steve to go ahead and set it up. Steve told Wells that the station had already approved a half hour time slot for Monday at 5:00 p.m. Both candidates would be given ten minutes to make a statement and then the disc jockey would ask a few questions of each participant for the final ten minutes. I, for one, will be listening to my radio Monday at 5:00 pm.

9/8/63

On the way to work today I noticed that both candidates had put out a few signs over the weekend. At work everyone was all a buzz about the upcoming radio appearances tonight by both. They both seemed a little nervous as neither had ever spoken live on the radio before. They joked back and forth and both seemed in great spirit today. As I was leaving work tonight I turned on my car radio and it was 5:00 p.m. and their time slot had just started. The announcer said that the two participants had flipped a coin and Wells had won the toss and had decided to speak first. He emphasized that he had been a sheriff's department deputy for many years and in that time he had built up relationships with many of the people in our county. He stated that he had much success in closing the majority of the cases that he had handled. He stated that there were no negative entries in his personnel file and he was sure that Sheriff Dolloff would give anyone who wanted one a fine reference as to his work performance. Wells ended and then Steve started to talk. He stated that he had solved all but one of the cases that had been assigned to him. He said that he hadn't the experience that Wells had, but that he had been quite active since becoming a detective and he felt that many people probably had read about a few of the happenings that he was involved in. He ended in saying that it has been a lifelong dream and goal of his to become the local sheriff and one of his greatest hopes is that someday that one case that has remained unsolved would be brought to closure. The announcer then asked a few questions to each candidate and I can't recall what those questions were. Both spoke well and presented themselves as being qualified for the job. If I didn't know both of these men it would be hard for me to choose between them. But, the fact that I consider Steve to be my best friend makes it easy to decide who I will be voting for.

9/13/63

Today is my eighteenth birthday. Mom bought the whole family lunch at the restaurant at Lincolnville Beach. It was a beautiful day and we took our shoes off and walked along the sandy beach looking for treasures before we ate. Brother Bob joined us. I had salmon for my meal and it was great. I hadn't had it in quite some time. Bob gave me the recently released album *The Free Wheelin' Bob Dylan*. It looks to be a good one, but I haven't played it yet. Mom and Terri got me a new winter coat and winter boots that I'll be needing in a few months. Also they got me a watch so I would never have an excuse to be late to work. Also tonight Sally took me out to eat at the pizza shop and then we went to the drive-in movies. I was off duty today as it's Saturday and was able to enjoy the day very much with the family and Sally. Tonight the drive-in closed down for the season. We saw *Cleopatra* and both of us enjoyed it. When I was dropping Sally off at her house she pulled a little box out of her jacket and handed it to me. I opened the box and it was a silver ring and she took it from my hand and pushed it onto my finger. She said that she had bought it at the Indian shop at the beach earlier this summer. I really like the ring as it is not fancy. It is just a basic silver ring with a brass border and it fit my finger perfectly. I told Sally that I would wear it always and gave her a kiss good night.

9/27/63

Today has been the worst day of my life. It started out well as Mom had called Bob last night and asked him to come up and he joined us at about 9:00 a.m. This being Saturday we had no problem as far as getting together. I felt something was wrong as Mom seemed very serious and direct and she did not seem to have the good humor that she usually has. After breakfast she asked the three of us to join her in the living room. Terri and I sat on the couch and Bob sat in Dad's easy chair. She didn't sit down and paced back and forth for a while. Most of the time her back was toward us and after a while I sensed that she was crying. I got up and went to her to try to comfort her and she said, "No Billy, please sit down." I did and she turned to us and started to speak. She told us that all good things end eventually. She said that she had put in her notice at the mill and would not be working there anymore. Bob asked her why she had done that. She told us that her health had been a problem and that she was no longer able to perform her duties in a satisfactory manner so she felt it was time to leave. She told us that she had been to see our doctor and he had done some tests on her. She continued and said that she also had seen a specialist who did even more extensive testing on her and both doctors agreed. She started really openly crying at that point and I yelled, "NO!!" without thinking of what I was doing. At that point she nodded to Bob and I and we understood what she was telling us. Terri didn't really understand and she asked Mom to explain. Mom came over to the couch and sat between Terri and I and hugged Terri. She told us that she had a cancer and it was a fast progressing one and that God and the angels would be coming for her soon. We were all in tears by this point and could not speak. Terri got up and ran up to her room. I was going to follow her to console her but Mom told me to give her a few minutes. Bob and I hugged Mom and she told us that the doctors gave her no more than two months to live. About ten minutes went by and all three of us went up and sat with Terri on her bed and hugged one another. Later in the day, after Bob left, I called Sally and gave her the bad news and immediately she offered to come over daily and sit with Mom so that Terri could go to school and I could go to work without worrying about her. We accepted Sally's kind offer as we all feel she is almost a member of our family at this point. Today was the worst day of my life and I can't imagine there will ever be a worse day coming, at least I hope not.

9/29/63

Sally came over today to stay with Mom. This was the first day she did this and she let me know that whenever we needed her that she'd surely be there to help. She added that she considers my mom to be a friend of hers and she enjoys being with her. Mom got up and got dressed before Sally arrived. Sally arrived around 7:30 a.m. which gave Terri and I plenty of time to get off to our day at work and school. As I left I assured Sally that I'd be only a phone call away if she needed me. She gave me a hug and assured me that they'd be fine. When I got home at about 5:15 p.m. Mom was eating. Sally had prepared soup and a sandwich for her. I drove Sally home and she said everything went fine today. She stated that they had played a lot of cards and watched some television. She said Mom had a nap this afternoon which lasted a couple of hours. She told me that her dad could drop her off at our house in the morning so I wouldn't have to pick her up. It is a great relief to our family what Sally is doing. I don't know what we'd do without her and I told her that as I dropped her off at her house.

10/4/63

Today, being Saturday, I was home with Mom and Terri. Sally didn't come over but she did call me this evening and told me she's noticed changes in Mom. I noticed changes too. She doesn't always get dressed in the morning now. At least half of her days are spent wearing pajamas and bundled up in her robe. The other day when Sally was with her she accidentally spilled some coffee on her pajama top and she asked Sally to go upstairs to her room and get another top out of her drawer and bring it to her. She did that and as Mom took off the wet top she noticed a very large black and blue welt on her back and neck area. She did not comment to Mom about what she had seen. This afternoon Mom asked Terri to go to her room and have a nap and she did lay down and slept for a couple of hours. While Terri slept Mom told me that she had opened savings accounts at the bank which will take care of us for a long time if we are thrifty with our money management. She told me that there was $30,000 each already deposited into the bank in Terri's, Bob's and my names. She handed me a card to fill out and sign and told me to take it to the bank and that would allow me to oversee Terri's activities on her account. She also handed me a check for $5000 and she told me that she wanted me to give it to Sally after she had passed away. I fought back tears when she gave me the check and told her I'd see to it that Sally got the check. It was made out to her. Mom asked me not to mention it to Sally until after she passed. She said that she wants very much to be able to die at home and not in some institution. She realized that if she did die at home it would be rough on us, especially Terri, but she said that she'd discuss this with her and hoped she'd understand. She told me she had received the money from the insurance policy that was on Dad's life when he died. She had received $100,000. I never knew this until she told me about it today. She pulled me over beside her on the couch and told me that I was a man now and that she had complete faith in me to raise Terri as she and Dad would have us raise her. She asked me to be a good and productive person in life and always to work with Bob to see that Terri is taken care of. By this time I was fully in tears, but nodded my head to her and assured her that her wishes would be done. I asked her if she were in any pain and she told me that it comes and goes. Just then Terri came running downstairs and joined Mom and I on the couch. We had a three hug and then watched TV for most of the remainder of the day. Mom had given me good news today and she had seen to it that we'd be taken care of in the years to come. Her comments to me told me that she felt I was now a grown-up and will be fully capable of taking care of Terri and myself from now on. I felt good about what she had said about me, but bad that she had to say it.

10/12/63

Mom told Terri today that she wishes to pass on here at our house. She told me that, surprisingly, Terri had accepted this thought and seemed to understand why Mom feels this way. I've noticed that she is losing weight and her appetite seems to be dwindling. While Terri was upstairs this afternoon Mom told me that she would like to be cremated and did not want to have a funeral. I told her I'd see to it that this was done. She said that she doubted that she'd ever leave the house again and that later on she'd like me to ask Pastor Mark of our church to come to see her. She told me, not yet, but in a couple of weeks she'd like him to come to visit her. Mom can still get on her feet and get to the bathroom but pain seems to be ever more evident as the days pass. I pray daily that her pain will be as minimal as possible and that she will not suffer. I also pray that Terri, Bob and I will be strong through this and be able to cope with life after she is gone.

10/19/63

It seems lately that I only get enough time on the weekends to write in my diary. Mom is still able to get to the bathroom by herself and she comes downstairs during the day. She never gets dressed anymore and always has her pajamas on. Bob came up today and we put the boat away for the season. We didn't use it much this year, but when we did go out they were very enjoyable times. Mom's last time out fishing will always be remembered. She enjoyed herself very much that day. We all ate lunch together and then Mom asked the three of us to join her in the living room. She told us that she had made out a will recently. She had it there to show us and had Sally witness her signature on it a few days ago. She asked me to deliver it to her attorney and I told her I would. She told us that the house and all of her belongings would be split up equally by her three children. She said it would be up to us how we distributed the assets between us. She told us that probably one of us would end up with the house eventually and the other two siblings would probably have their share bought out by the one who was to remain in the home. She said she was leaving those affairs up to us as she truly didn't want to be bothered with them at this point. Bob and I assured her that we would divide things up fairly and that all three of us would be happy with the final outcome. Mom told Bob that she feels that I am a man now and she feels that I can take care of myself and Terri here at the house. She told him also that Sally was here often and is a big help when she is here. Bob then talked about an hour with Mom and they were more or less alone during their conversation. After that, Bob gave us all a big hug and left. I could see he was quite emotional as he walked out of the door. And, indeed he should be, as it is possible that he might never see Mom again alive.

10/26/63

Mom told Terri and I today that she had forgotten to tell us the other day when the family was talking about her will that the house is free and clear and has no mortgage or attachments on it. Her spirits remain good, but I feel that her pain is increasing both in intensity and frequency. We are lucky in that we have a bathroom both upstairs and down and Mom is still able to take care of her bodily functions without help. The talk at work this week, and of course the jokes, all seemed to center around the upcoming election. It is my opinion that Steve is a slightly better candidate than Wells, but our county certainly can't go wrong with either of these fine men leading the way. We are all anxious for the election to be over and done with. The new sheriff will not take the reins of office until the first of the year. As I stated before, I feel it will be a very close election.

11/3/63

I drove Sally home tonight when I got home. When we arrived at her house she asked me to turn the car off as she wanted to talk to me. I did so and, all of a sudden, she seemed really serious. She looked me straight in the eyes and said, "Your Mom told me today that her biggest regret is that she will not be around to see us get married." I didn't know what to say, but I did get a little misty around the eyes. She continued, "I've thought long and hard about this today and as far as I'm concerned she can see us get married. I know that we could not get her to the church, Billy, but we could get married right here in your house, that is if you want me as your wife." I smiled and told her that there is nothing that I would rather do. I told her that I would be over to see her dad tomorrow night and if he approved then we should go ahead and get married. She gave me a hug and a big kiss and said that she'd tell her dad that I would be over tomorrow evening to see him. She said she would not indicate to him what I want to talk about. Tonight as I write this in my bedroom I feel that it is probably too early for us to get married. We are both young and relatively inexperienced when it comes to setting up housekeeping. I do love Sally very much, but, if it wasn't for one fact, I'd probably decide not to get married at this point. That one fact or aspect is Mom and her wishes. I feel that it is probable that in the near future I will have to own up for my grave error and I will undoubtedly be incarcerated at that time. Everything tells me not to get married as it would not be fair to Sally to do that. But, my Mom has been hurt far too much in her life and I will not be the one to prevent her from being able to see what, to her, is her final wish come true.

11/4/63

Mr. Slater called me at work today and said that he'd be glad to come over to our house this evening. He said that he realizes that we want to keep an eye on Mom and that there would be no inconvenience in his coming over. I told him that I appreciated that and looked forward to seeing him tonight. I got home about 5:30 and I told Mom and Sally that Mr. Slater would be coming over to see me tonight. Mom asked Sally to have dinner with us and she did after calling home and telling her mom what her plans were. Mr. Slater arrived around 6:30 and I asked him to join me upstairs in my room. In one way the things I said to him in the next fifteen minutes or so were the hardest things ever for me to verbalize. In another way however they were the easiest things that I have ever said. I told him that I love Sally very much. I stated that she has told me that she loves me equally as much. I continued by saying that, although we both could probably continue our education in college, we have decided that we'd like to go to work and set up housekeeping together and to get married. I told him we would not do this without the consent of he and Mrs. Slater. I added that we realize that we are very young and most people would think that we are too young to develop a lasting marriage. I told him that most people would be correct in thinking negatively about this, but they'd be forgetting one key aspect. They'd be forgetting that Sally and I love each other very much! I told him that financially Mom has seen to it that all three siblings would be taken care of and after the first part of December both Sally and I would have full-time year-round employment. Mr. Slater smiled at me and told me he was very proud of me. He said that when I had asked to speak with him that he felt it would be concerning marriage. It was no surprise to him. He stood up and shook my hand and told me he would take our wishes into consideration and he would discuss it fully with Mrs. Slater and would give us an answer, probably tomorrow. We walked downstairs and Sally immediately walked over to her father and gave him a big hug. He stuck his head into the living room and talked to Mom briefly and then he and Sally left. I hope and pray that I expressed myself in a good fashion to him and that he and Mrs. Slater will smile on our wishes and allow them to happen.

11/5/63

At work today all I could think of was what would Mr. and Mrs. Slater's decision would be. I was hoping that Mr. Slater would call me tonight and give me their answer. Sally and I have not told anyone about our wishes. I received a call from a lady in town and she stated she just saw a very drunk man hitchhiking up near the library. I voiced out a message to Deputy Wells and he said he'd handle it. In two minutes Wells was at the location, but the man was nowhere in sight. He drove around the adjacent streets but could not locate the man. Apparently he had been picked up by a trusting soul and he was on his way home to sleep it off. Just then, at about 11:15 a.m., Mr. Slater arrived at the department. He asked to speak to me and I asked the deputy at our check-in window to let him in. I walked down the hall to greet him and asked him to join me at my work station. He told me that he did not want to disrupt our office business, but he felt that he should see me personally today. I told him that was fine and that it was not a problem. He then smiled at me and shook my hand and told me that their family has agreed to give their blessing and that Sally and I can get married now with their approval. I thanked him and told him that their decision means more to me than anyone could realize. He then left as quickly as he had arrived. Mr. and Mrs. Slater are truly class acts and I will be lucky in a few days to be able to call them my mother and father-in-law. With all that is happening in my life right now it slipped my mind to state that yesterday was election day. I did get Steve to go up and vote. He wasn't going to as his mother suggested that people never should vote for themselves. He did however and we found out today that he had won the election by four votes. Deputy Wells was asked if he wanted there to be a recount and he said no. He stated that he was sure that the election officials are great at counting and he was satisfied with the outcome. My best friend will become the new sheriff at the start of next year. The competitors shook hands in the office and this election was over. We were all very happy that it was.

11/10/63

I got home from work today and while driving Sally home she told me that Mom was really slipping fast with her health. She finds it very hard now to get up and down our flight of stairs. She told Sally that she felt that very soon, perhaps tomorrow, she would start staying in her room on a full-time basis. I suggested to Sally that we have the wedding in our home so that Mom would get her wish and be able to see us get married. I told her we could have the ceremony on Sunday the 16th if that was okay with her. She said it would be and she stated that she wants Terri to be her maid of honor. I felt that was a wonderful thing for her to want to do and assured her that Terri will be honored. Sally said that she was going to wear her mother's wedding dress as it fits her and it's still in really good condition. I told her that I would call Steve tonight and see if he wanted to be my best man. Sally said she'd call our pastor to see if he'd be available Sunday at 4:00 p.m. to officiate. She said she'd ask her mom to help make some sandwiches and finger foods that we could snack on after the ceremony. I dropped Sally off at her house and came home and called Steve. He was quite surprised, but said that he'd gladly be my best man. We have a piano in the living room so I decided to call Connie Partridge, who is our pianist at church, and she said she'd be very glad to attend and play the wedding march for us. Then, I went downstairs and made it official. I told Mom that Sally and I would be getting married on Sunday at 4:00 p.m. and I told her, jokingly, to be there or be square! At this point she started to cry and I held her in my arms for quite a while. Our house is not really big and I realize that it will be quite full with people on Sunday. I hope and pray that Mom will still be with us then.

11/11/63

Mom did not come downstairs today. She spent most of the day in bed and never got out of her pajamas. Sally told me that Mom read quite a lot and watched a little TV on the small set she has on top of her bureau. Sally played cards with her and they did a lot of talking during the day. After lunch Mom drifted off and had a nap for a couple of hours. Sally told me that their friendship increases daily and that she is really going to miss her when she passes. She is still able to make it to the bathroom on her own and can take care of her business in there. When I got home Sally and I talked to Mom in her room while Terri was downstairs watching cartoons on TV. The three of us decided that when things get really bad for Mom that Terri should go over and stay with her Aunt Barbara for a few days. Sally told me that Barb has been coming over and helping periodically and she has especially been helpful in keeping Terri occupied and keeping her mind off Mom. Before I went up to bed tonight I called Bob and suggested that he might want to ask for some time off from his work and get home for a while. He told me that he had planned on doing that and that he'd be home Thursday night after he gets out of work. He stated that he hoped to be able to stay with us until Mom passes, but he did not know definitely whether he could or not at this point. I peeked into Terri's room and she was sound asleep and then went in to say goodnight to Mom. She asked me to pray with her and I pulled a chair up beside her bed and folded my hands around hers and I said a prayer and then she said her prayer. I asked if I could get her anything and she said no, that she was all set. I gave her a kiss and went off to bed.

11/13/63

Bob arrived tonight as planned. He had packed a suitcase. He'll be sleeping in his room that we've kept pretty much as it was when he moved out. His room is on one side of Mom's and mine is on the other side of her so we can hear her easily if she calls us. She did not get out of bed at all yesterday or today other than going across the hallway to the bathroom a couple of times. She eats very little now and has lost a lot of weight. She still has her good humor, but we can sense that she has pain often and sometimes it is excruciating. While I was wishing her goodnight this evening I suggested that we could have the wedding upstairs in her room and with some folks in the hallway. What she said in response to me I will never forget. She said, "No Billy, I will try hard to be able to come downstairs. If I'm unable to make it down there I want everyone to stay downstairs and enjoy themselves. I will be up here in bed and I can hear what goes on very well. Your Dad will be here right beside me and we'll both listen together and we will be very, very happy!" I did ask the sheriff today if he'd like to attend and he said he wouldn't miss it for the world. Sally told me that Mom had asked her to pull out her beautiful purple dress from her closet and iron it up a little for her and she had done so. Both Sally and I feel that it is very unlikely that Mom will be able to join us downstairs.

11/15/63

Needless to say, none of us slept very well tonight. I stayed up until about midnight and finally nodded off. It took Mom, Terri and Bob quite some time to get to sleep. Everyone is very excited! I will be married tomorrow! Mom has been confined to her bed for days now and only gets up to go to the bathroom. I hope and pray that all goes well tomorrow.

11/16/63

Wow!! Today was a great, great day!! We all woke up about 7:00 a.m., except Mom. We let her sleep and she didn't awake until almost 9:00 a.m. Bob brought coffee and a doughnut up to her for her breakfast; it was all that she wanted. Just about 9:00 a.m. the whole Slater family, except Sally, showed up and wanted to help with the preparations for the day. They brought plenty of sandwiches and finger foods which we packed into the refrigerator. Mrs. Slater reminded me that it is bad luck for a groom to see a potential bride before the wedding event on the day of the marriage. She said Sally was having her hair done and would be here at about 3:00 p.m. to make her final preparations. She stated that when she arrives that she wants me to go to my room and close the door until she gets upstairs into Mom's room where she'll put her dress on. We all then went about cleaning up the place and making our living room look as much like the inside of a church as possible. The pastor told us he'd bring his podium and we could set it on a small table at the end of the room near the piano and he could officiate from it. By 11:00 a.m. we had things pretty well cleaned and set up so the Slaters left and said they'd be back around 3:00, this time with Sally. I went upstairs to see what Mom wanted for lunch and she said she wasn't hungry. She said she might eat a bit after the wedding. I held her hand. She told me that she was very proud of me and then she drifted off to sleep. While Mom was sleeping I went into my room and had a nap also. Bob never has a nap and he was playing with Terri downstairs. I woke up about 2:00 p.m. Mom was still asleep. Connie Partridge was the first person to show up and she arrived a little after 3:00 p.m. She went into the living room and practiced playing on our piano which she had never played before. The music sounded especially nice today and we seldom have anyone who can really play it in our home anymore. Dad used to play and it was his piano. Just then the Slaters' car came into the driveway and I almost forgot to go upstairs to my room. I wanted to see Sally so badly, but I did trundle off to my room and closed my door. I heard Sally come upstairs and was surprised that she came up alone. She went into Mom's room and closed the door and then I heard Mom say, "Okay Billy, you can come out now!" I think everyone in the house laughed when they heard that! Just then Steve arrived and he had brought three small benches that he had borrowed from our baseball coach that he said we might set up in the living room to serve as pews. I told him that was a great idea and we moved them inside and set them up. He asked me if I was nervous and I told him that surprisingly I wasn't. I said that I had been ready for this moment for a while now and have looked forward to it. At a little after 3:30 people started to arrive. Aunt Barbara and Uncle Ben arrived and had brought presents. We hadn't thought about presents so I asked Steve if he would set up our card table near the entrance of the living room and he did in case more gifts were in the offing. He said that he'd be glad to welcome people and escort them into the living room and get them seated. I told him not too many people would be attending and most of them had already arrived. I hadn't seen Terri around for a while and I asked Bob where she was and he told me she was upstairs helping Sally to get ready and putting on her own pretty dress as well. I asked Bob to go upstairs and go to my room and he'd see a pretty bouquet of red and white roses that I had purchased yesterday in a vase on my chest of drawers. I asked him to give it to Terri and she could carry it with her when the ceremony began. I then went out to our garage and brought in two beautiful bouquets of flowers that I also had purchased yesterday, and I placed one on each side of the location where we'd be giving our vows. The flowers were still beautiful and aromatic. Just then Sheriff Dolloff arrived and Al Clewley came through the door at the same time. We weren't expecting Al, but were glad that he came. Connie's music sounded great. I pretty much mingled with folks, but spent most of my time with the Slaters. Mr. Slater pulled out a very fine old pocket watch from his suit coat and handed it to me. He said his father had given it to him and he wanted me to have it. I shook his hand and gave him a hug and thanked him. I have a feeling that the watch is quite valuable and it still keeps perfect time even after all those years. Now it was about 3:50 p.m. and three girls from our school class showed up and joined us. Sally had invited them and they are her best friends. Our Pastor had arrived and set up his podium. I asked Mrs. Slater to go upstairs to see if Sally and Terri were ready. I told Connie that everyone that I thought would be attending had arrived. And now it had arrived, the most important moment of my life. It was 4:00. Mrs. Slater came back downstairs and told us that everyone was ready. I shook a few hands and went to the front of the room with Steve at my side. Mr. Slater stood beside Steve as he was to be giving Sally away. I smiled at everyone, took a deep breath, and nodded to Connie to start the wedding march. First to come downstairs was Terri and she had the pretty bouquet in her hands. She moved slowly and was very serious in her appearance, but she was just beautiful. She came to the front of the room and stood near where Sally would join her shortly. Connie kept playing and then, at the top of the stairs, we all saw a sight that I'm sure I will never forget. Sally and Mom were arm in arm at the top of the stairs looking more beautiful by far than I had ever seen them! There wasn't a dry eye in the house as they walked down over those stairs. Mom had her beautiful purple floor-length dress on and Sally had her mom's wedding dress on which looked fabulous. No one had expected Mom to be able to attend the ceremony; nobody except Mom herself. Pastor then asked who is giving this lady away and Mr. Slater said that he was. He then turned to Sally and asked her if she took me to be her lawfully wedded husband and she said a few prepared words and then said that she did take me to be her husband. Pastor turned his eyes to me and asked if I take Sally to be my lawfully wedded wife and I said a few words that came totally out of the air and from my heart and ended by saying that I do take Sally to be my lawfully wedded wife. Pastor then asked if anyone knew of any reason that this wedding should not occur and nobody had any objection. By 4:15 I was giving Sally the first public kiss that I had ever given her and we were married! We then set out the snacks and sandwiches for everyone and we opened our presents. Mom stayed downstairs and sat on the couch and socialized and seemed to have a wonderful time today. By 7:00 p.m. everyone had left. Sally had not left and would be staying with me from now on. Her family gave her a big hug and kiss as they left and there were tears flowing. I helped Mom up to her room and thanked her very much for making what I realized to be a supreme effort today in attending our wedding. She told me that she wouldn't have missed it for the world. Sally and I had discussed it earlier that we would sleep in different beds until Mom passed. Sally slept tonight in my bed and I slept on the couch in the living room. Today was, and will be I'm sure, the most memorable day of my life.

11/18/63

I got home from work tonight and noticed a real turn for the worst in Mom's appearance. She still had a smile on her face and joked with us from time to time, but she seemed to have gone into a shutdown mode which told us that she realized that her end would be coming soon. She stayed in bed all day except for going to the bathroom. She still was able to handle her business once she got to the toilet, but Bob said that he had to help her to be able to walk to and from it. A nurse friend of mine once told me that the way to tell if a person's body is shutting down is to feel their feet. If you find them to be cold then that person will more than likely die shortly. I felt Mom's feet and they were still warm. She kind of giggled and wanted me to stop tickling her. I laughed and never explained to her what I was doing. After dinner we all sat with her in her room. She told us that Auntie Barbara had been over to see her today and she asked if Terri can come over to visit her for a few days. At first thought Terri seemed excited and seemed to like the idea as she loves her Aunt Barb. Then she thought a little more and she asked Mom if she should go as she really will miss her. Mom said it was okay to go and in fact Bob had packed some of her clothes for her today into her little suitcase and she was all set to go. Mom then asked me to drive Terri over to Barb's house. Terri gave Mom a hug and a kiss and picked up her suitcase and we headed downstairs. As I opened the door to go outside Terri dropped the suitcase and turned and ran upstairs yelling, "Mom, Mom!!" She ran to Mom and shouted, "Mommie, Mom, I love you!! I love you very, very much!" The tears were coming down all of our cheeks and Mom hugged her for a long while and kissed them away. She looked at Terri straight in her eyes and pointed to Terri's heart and then to her head. She said, "Terri, I will always be here and I will always be here also and you will always be in my mind and heart as well. Now Aunt Barb is waiting for you and I think she has a surprise for you when you get over to see her." Mom gave her one more big, big, hug and kiss and I took Terri by the hand and we walked down over the stairs. As I opened the door to leave Terri yelled up to Mom, "Mom you are the best mom in the world and I love you!!" Mom yelled down to Terri, "Have fun!!" I then dropped Terri off at her Aunt's house and returned home. As I came through the door Bob's eyes and mine met and we both knew, without having to discuss it, what Mom's decision as to where Terri should be meant. Although Terri is very young I feel that there is a slight realization in her mind that she may never see Mom again alive. Terri is very smart and intuitive and she is the light of all of our lives.

11/20/63

When I got home this evening Sally and Bob whispered to me that Mom was really failing today. They both felt that her end was fast approaching. I took her supper upstairs to her, but all she ate was the applesauce. I did get her to drink a little grape juice, but she showed very little interest in food. She told me that she was pretty sure that her time had come. She mentioned to all three of us that we were to take good care of Terri always. We assured her that we would. She asked me to tell Terri periodically how much she loved her and hoped that she would never forget this. She also stated to me to tell Terri, Bob and Sally how proud she was of them and to never let them forget that. She then looked me straight in the eyes and said, "I'm sure I don't have to tell you how I feel about you." She started crying at that point and I cried right along with her. I hugged her until she regained her composure. She was right; she did not need to tell me how she felt about me. Her whole life has been a testament to that. The three of us decided that we'd take turns tonight sitting with Mom as she slept. I told Bob that I'd take the first watch and I'd wake him up later to take my place. I read Mom a few of the passages of The Bible before she drifted off to sleep. The last thing that she heard from me was the 23rd Psalm which is her favorite. I never did wake Bob or Sally up to take my place. I just sat in a chair next to Mom and held her hand as we both fell asleep and the night closed in around us.

11/21/63

I awoke around 5:30 a.m. and it was over. Mom had passed away. I was still holding her hand. I straightened her hair and kissed her forehead and sat quietly beside her until I stopped crying. I'm glad that I was with her at the end and also glad that I was holding her hand. I stood up and left her room and woke up Sally and Bob. They could tell by looking at me that it was over. They gave me a big hug and went into Mom's room. I went downstairs and never saw Mom again. After a while they came down and I told Bob that the best thing for me right now is to keep busy so I planned to go to work. He and Sally said that they'd call the funeral home and have Mom picked up. Her wish was to be cremated and to have no service. Bob said he'd see to it. I asked them if they would pick up Terri today from her aunt's and bring her home. I told Bob that I didn't feel that I had it in me to tell Terri that Mom had died. He said he would tell her today. I got my uniform on and hugged them both and drove off to work. Bob told me he would have to go back home this afternoon as he had to get back to his job. He said he'd probably be gone by the time I got home. I don't remember a thing about what happened today at work except I finally decided, now that Mom had passed, to own up to the biggest mistake that I'd ever made. The staff at the office couldn't believe that I came to work today. They said I should have called in and stayed home with my family. I told them in my case that it is best that I remain active and work is beneficial to me right now. At lunch time I did ask Dolloff if I could take a few extra minutes as I had some business to attend to. He told me to take as long as I needed as we had plenty of coverage in my department today. I had brought this diary along and decided I'd make a few last entries into it. I drove down a side street near the harbor where I would not be disturbed and made this entry:

On September 7, 1961, I made the biggest mistake of my life. I am very sorry for what I did that night. My mother was working late that evening and I had gone up behind the mill and was waiting for her to come out of the back door as she always does. I was hiding in the woods and was going to surprise her. It was already dark and I could see Leaky Boots working on the top floor. He was almost always the last to leave at the end of each day. After waiting for about a half hour Mom came out of the door and Rance Edwards was right behind her. What I should have done right then was to come out of hiding and walk Mom home. I waited a little too long and then saw a scene that I will never forget. Rance quickly caught up to Mom and pulled her to him and tried to kiss her. I could tell by his speech that he had been drinking that day and he was clearly very drunk. Mom tried to push him away and, had she been successful, Rance could still be living today. She was not successful and Rance then pawed and groped her and put his hands where you should not touch a lady. I was livid but just before I stepped out of the woods to help her it was over. Mom kicked Rance in his groin and hurried down the driveway and was gone. Rance called her every foul word that he could remember in his drunken state as she went out of sight. He had fallen down onto the tarred parking area and writhed in agony for a minute or so. He then got up and got into his car and drove off looking for Mom. He never found her. I was incredulous over what had just happened and even more incredulous that I had not gone to Mom's aid. I ran across the field behind the mill and believe that no one saw me at all while I was there.

I thought and fumed and decided that this could never happen again. I knew that I had to go see Rance and eliminate this as a problem. I walked over past our house and saw that Mom had gotten home. Aunt Barbara, who had been with Terri, had already left. No one saw me as I passed the house. I then walked through the woods up toward Rance's camp. It sits in the forest beneath the mountains that lie behind and to the north of our town. A dirt road goes into the camp from Route 1, but I did not use that road. I travelled only through the woods. There were no clouds that evening and the moon was pretty much full so I could see very well. I take full responsibility for my actions on that evening and, again, I am very sorry for what I did. I then signed my comments William Allen Todd and dated it 11/21/63.

I headed back to work and at the end of the day I asked Sheriff Dolloff if I could see him tonight regarding a very important matter. He said sure and asked me to join him at his camp this evening. He said he was going to try to burn some brush outside, but we could pull up a couple of lawn chairs and maybe the fire would keep us warm. I told him I'd join him after dinner. Sally had prepared spaghetti and meatballs for our first meal together as a threesome. Bob had already left. Sally told me that Bob had told Terri about Mom and that she initially took the news very hard. She had cried for a very, very long time, but the cry had been truly what she needed and she was now doing a lot better. After we ate I stood up and told the girls that I had to go out for a while and was going to see Dolloff. As I was leaving Terri came over to me and asked, "Can I stay up until you get home?" Normally I would have said no to her, but considering the hard day that we had had, I told her that it was okay. I decided to walk to Dolloff's camp which is located at the base of the mountain that lies behind our town. Actually it is only about a mile from Rance's camp if you walk to it through the woods. Dolloff's is located about two miles from our house. I brought with me a backpack and inside was this diary. I reached his camp about 7:30 p.m. and he was sitting outside keeping an eye on two burn piles. I pulled up a lawn chair and joined him. The heat from the blazes kept us good and warm. He asked me what I wanted to talk about. I opened the backpack and handed him my diary. I told him he should read what I had written in the book today. He looked at me and said, "Billy, are you sure that you want to do this?" I told him that I was sure and that I wanted to own up to a mistake that I had made several years ago. He opened the diary and leafed to the back of the book and slowly read all of what I've written in it today. After he finished reading it he closed the book and stared for some time down at the ground in front of him. He did not speak for what seemed to be an eternity, but finally he turned to me and said, "I have always felt that it might have been you Bill that did in Rance, but I guess I just hoped beyond hope that I was wrong." He shook his head and we both just sat there and did a lot of thinking but did not speak at all for quite some time. He then looked at me and broke the silence by saying, "Bill, you know that this puts us both in a real bind don't you?" I told him that I knew that it did. We sat and thought some more and then I decided that I owed it to Dolloff and to everyone involved to tell the complete truth. I stated, "Sheriff, what happened that night was that I walked through the woods to Rance's cabin. I really had no plan, but I knew that I had to talk to Rance and make it clear to him that he should never again harass my mother. As I was nearing the hill that slopes down to his camp I heard a gunshot. I ducked down behind a tree and watched with amazement as my mother came out of the camp and quickly ran down the dirt road that leads to Route 1. I didn't say a thing to her. I waited for a couple of minutes and then walked down the slope to the camp. I could hear the television was on. I stepped inside and found Rance deceased on the kitchen floor. He had been shot in the head. There looked to have been an altercation and I assumed that Rance had attacked Mom again and she must have grabbed one of the weapons off his kitchen table and pulled the trigger. I didn't have time to think at all. All I wanted to do was to protect my mom at all costs. I picked up the pistol that was on the floor and put it into a burlap sack that I found also on the floor. Luckily I spotted Mom's change purse under the kitchen table. I stuffed it into my jacket. It must have fallen out of her jacket during the melee. Then I quickly ran up the slope and again through the woods and I took the sack containing the pistol down behind our high school and threw it deeply into the woods. I had felt that no one would find the pistol for quite some time if at all, but I didn't realize that Steve was tenting down there that night. After tossing the burlap sack I quickly ran home. Mom and Terri had already gone to bed. I located the jacket that she wears most of the time to work and put the purse inside one of her pockets. I did not want to consider my mother to be a murderer so I rationalized that she surely must have had a good reason for her actions. Rance must have attacked her. The only thing I didn't know was why Mom had gone to the camp. I decided that I didn't really care why and also decided never to discuss that night with Mom. Dolloff thought for a minute and then said, "Leaky Boots stated when we questioned him about that night that he had seen and heard the hubbub that occurred behind the mill from an upper level window. Before he could get downstairs to break it up it was all over and both Rance and your mother were gone. Then he noticed what appeared to be a young boy cross the field behind the mill. He could not tell who it was and only stated that the boy moved fast and was out of sight quickly." Dolloff then asked me to sit and watch the fires as he wanted to go into his camp and think for a while. After about ten minutes he came back out and sat down beside me. He turned and looked into my eyes and said these words that I'll never forget, "Billy if you can forget, forever, what happened that night and never mention it to me or anyone else again then you can leave right now and get home to your young family who need you. You should take with you this diary and I would suggest that you destroy it." I sat and was contemplating whether I'd be able to never again discuss that night with anyone and then Dolloff cleared my mind of all negativity by saying, "Bill, this offer only lasts for one more minute. If you are not up and on your way within the next minute then I'll have to take you to the sheriff's department."

In the next five seconds I rose to my feet, shook Dolloff's hand, and started running as fast as I could down his driveway. I realized that Dolloff's words and actions were telling me to go and sin no more. They were telling me to be a good man in life and to take care of my family. He was allowing me to walk away from the felony of tampering with homicidal evidence which, depending on which side of the bed my judge would get out on, my sentencing day could have landed me in prison for five and maybe as much as fifteen years. One of the chief law enforcement officers in our county gave me a pass and let me go. I realized then and there that I will do the very best I can to walk a straight and narrow path and strive to be the best person that I can be, always. I also realized and made a commitment to myself never to discuss this matter again with anyone. I did not stop running until I reached home. Sally and Terri were still awake. They wondered why I was so sweaty. I told them I ran all the way from Dolloff's camp. Sally asked me if she could get me some ice cream and I told her I'd love to have some. She scooped some out for me and I sat at the kitchen table and thought over what had just happened. The two girls had gone into the living room and were eating ice cream sitting on the floor while watching the 11:00 p.m. news on TV. I watched them. They looked very cute sitting there side by side. I hollered in to them, "What's on the news tonight?" Terri said, "President Kennedy is flying around!" I gazed out the kitchen window and down the dark street. I realized that JFK has been a very good president and we sure are lucky to have him as our leader. I also realized that, had I been old enough to vote, that I probably would not have voted for him. I picked up my dish of ice cream and went into the living room and sat on the couch behind the girls. They were intently watching the President and Jackie on the screen. I asked, "Where are they?" After a minute or so Sally piped up saying, "Apparently they are on a campaign tour and are flying around Texas today." She added, "I think they are flying to Dallas tomorrow." I sat there and gave thought to the things that have happened over the last few years to my family. We surely have had some rough times. Terri, considering Mom's passing, is in pretty good humor tonight. I

94

don't think that she truly understands yet that our mom is gone. Well, I feel that our luck is about to improve and that all of the bad news is behind us now. I look forward to better and brighter days to come. Sally got up and came over and joined me on the couch. Then Terri got up and walked over and looked up to us and said, "Are you going to be my parents now?" Sally looked at me and saw that I was getting emotional and finding it hard to speak and she pulled Terri to her and looked into her eyes and said, "We'd love to do that!" Terri hugged us both and gave us one of her Terri smiles, the kind that only she can give. At that moment she looked so like our mom. I stood up and took her by her hand and walked her upstairs. It was way past her bedtime.

About the Author

Dave Dodd moved to mid-coast Maine 65 years ago with his family. He attended grade school in Lincolnville and graduated from Camden High School in 1965.

Dave then served for two years in the U.S. Army and was stationed in Germany. He worked for all of his life at various jobs in the mid-coastal area. He had the honor of being the deputy district governor of the Lions Club at one time.

Dave has felt for all of his life that he has been on a vacation in our beautiful state.

www.ingramcontent.com/pod-product-compliance
Lightning Source LLC
Chambersburg PA
CBHW030355180626
46812CB00007B/2895

*9 7 8 1 9 4 3 4 2 4 2 6 9 *